Isle *of* Man

Fear agus déithe

Men and gods

Title: Isle of Man, *Fear agus déithe (Men and Gods)*

Authors: John and Lottie Christian

Publisher: Lily Publications Ltd

Ramsey

Isle of Man

British Isles

www.lilypublications.co.uk

ISBN: 978-1-911177-11-1

Edition: First

A part of net proceeds from the sale of this work will be donated to: Manx National Heritage

Douglas, Isle of Man, IM1 3LY

Disclaimer:

This is a work of fiction. Names, characters, places, and incidents either are products of the author's imagination or are used fictitiously. Any resemblance to actual events or locales or persons, living or dead, is entirely coincidental. This is not a history book. Dates and events imagined in this work are not to be construed as historically accurate.

Dedication

Our journey together has been one filled with many challenges and opportunities, giving us a history of lessons by which we learned about love and compassion, not just for each other and our family, but also for those we have met along life's path. Our hope is our children, grandchildren, and the generations that follow, will find life and love just as amazing as we have. This book is dedicated to our remarkable daughters, the good men they married, and our delightful grandchildren.

— The authors

Acknowledgement

The authors graciously recognize and appreciate the work of Viktor Emil Frankl (26 March 1905 – 2 September 1997). Frankl was an Austrian neurologist and psychiatrist as well as a Holocaust survivor. His best-selling book, *Man's Search for Meaning*, was a tremendous inspiration to us.

Preface

Isle of Man is an intriguing philosophical novel about the tenacity, resilience, vengeance, and empathy of mankind in an ever-changing world, as well as how political and religious revisionism may have impacted and influenced civilizations throughout the ages.

Two intertwined stories containing vivid dream sequences and sensual poetry make this novel one that is sure to captivate your imagination and show how love and understanding can transcend the hands of time.

Dealing with recent tragic news about his wife, Christian must travel to the Isle of Man to retrieve her belongings. On his journey, he interacts with several interesting characters all dealing with various life-changing events; each faced with making choices that will determine how their path winds next.

Fin and Oshin

(Also Fin as Oshin)

Fin and Oshin went out to hunt,
Fal, lal, lo, as fal, lal, la.
With a noble train of men and dogs,
Not less in number than one hundred men,
So swift of foot and keen, none were their like;
With scores of Bandogs fierce they sallied forth,
O'er Hill and Dale, much Havock for to make.

Whom left they then at home but youthful Gorry!
Who slept secure beneath the shadowy rock;
Full three score Greyhounds, with their whelps, they left,
With three score lovely maidens young and fair,
As many old dames to attend the young.

Says Fin's fair daughter, in Disdain and Scorn,
"How on young Gorry shall we be revenged?"

Says Oshin's Daughter:
"Fast to the Harrows we will tie his Hair,
And to his nimble feet we'll set a train of Fire."

Then up starts Gorry, with a nimble spring,
Feeling his feet abroiling with the heat,
With Curses direful, vowing to destroy,
Those who presum'd t' affront a King his Son!
Swearing most bitterly by Sun and Moon,
To burn themselves and all their habitations,

Then to the Mountains hides he fast away,
His heavy Gorse-hack poised upon his shoulders.
Eight ponderous burthens thence he carried off,
And eight large Faggots cram'd in ilka Burthen.
Not eight such men as in the world are now
Could from the Ground one of these burthens raise.
Into each Window, he a Burthen thrust,
Into each Door, a Burthen of the same,
But the grand blazing Burthen on the floor
Of the great Hall he laid, and set on fire.

Meanwhile, our Heroes, Fin and Oshin hight,
They and their hardy men pursued the chase,
Eager, in sweat and dust all cover'd o'er.

Vast clouds full floating from the west
Were seen, like Billows dreadful, as I ween.

Then Fin he ran, and Oshin also ran,
Till faint and out of breath, he sat him down:
But Fin, the hardy chief, still held it out.
Then lift he up his lamentable Voice,
Calling to Oshin, who was far behind,
"We've nothing left but rueful, ruin'd walls!"

This mischief who has done? Who but young Gorry,
Who fled, and in a rocky Cavern hid himself.
Then chok'd with Smoke, they drag him by the heels,
And tore him Limb from Limb with Horses wild.

— *Traditional Manx Poem*

Chapter One

Countless, agonizing images invade the recesses of my mind, taunting me as I lay masked in darkness with too much time to think and little urge to sleep. Sleep has become my enemy, opening a door into my subconscious, replaying painful memories swirling around in my head in a dance with fantasy. What is real and was, or was not, real haunts my slumber-starved soul.

I shiver as I push back the heavy woolen blanket and crawl out of this unfamiliar bed. Sliding my icy feet into welcoming slippers, I pull on my bathrobe and tie the cloth belt snugly. Aided only by a sliver of light creeping in from beneath the door, I cautiously work my way to a modest desk no bigger than a nightstand, fumble for a dangling brass chain and pull it, sending a charge, illuminating a dim incandescent bulb shrouded in part by a green glass shade. The stillness of this wee hour is broken as I drag a small stool from beneath the desk, legs screeching in friction with the wooden floor. Sitting in the shadows, listening to the steady rhythm of waves gently splashing against the ship's hull eases my anguished mind. A fond recollection from many years past emerges . . . *She and I are standing together on a shore, watching lights from the distant city across the bay glisten brightly on placid water, casting illusions of candle flames flickering in the breeze. The bay is calm on this warm autumn evening. The familiar scent of fish, seaweed, and salt, mixed by the ocean, and the gentle cascading of the incoming tide, has lulled us into a serene mood. Kind expressions and gentle gestures resonate between us. Past conversation and memories are mutually sensed, stirring a feeling of elation in our souls. Proud of myself for having surprised her with yet another romantic outing, I gaze deep into her gentle blue eyes, present her with a yellow rose, her favorite, and we embrace tenderly. With fingers entwined, we lean against our old blue Chevy; our faithful transport on so many adventures. In hushed whispers, we reminisce about earlier outings, recalling how, once, we playfully danced between waves washing along the shore of Lake Erie, writing our names on a canvas of sand. We laugh, remembering those funny rubber duck suits we wore as we ventured under Niagara Falls on our honeymoon. Then, the trip we took the very next year, touring Gillette Castle in Connecticut with baby number one in tow, struggling with the stroller on all those rugged steps. And now, here we are, entranced by the beautiful city across the bay, lights burning brightly.*

A soft cry interrupts the serenity of the moment. We glance at each other with tepid amusement looking into a half-opened car window at two car seats, each cradling a soft, innocent bundle. The whimpering of one startles the other and the two begin a harmonious plea for attention. A cracker for the older and a bottle for the younger are the wages paid to resume peace, if only temporarily. The tide pushes the waves closer to us as the sun's reddish-orange glow chases the horizon, then swiftly disappears into the night. A cool breeze drifts across the bay, bringing with it the salty mist of the waves, dampening our skin. She shivers and leans into me so close, filling my senses with her familiar fragrance. For a moment, we are in a place where time has no meaning.

Cruelly, the gentle splashing of waves changes abruptly, pulling me away from fantasy, back to the reality of this moment and the purpose of my journey. I inhale deeply to see if I can still sense her near me; but the memory has faded, leaving my soul empty, ever hungry for another. *Do the gods hate me so much they would steal my precious remembrances of her?*

In the shadows of this strange dank space, I open my journal, raise my pen, and begin to write.

Wednesday, March 15, 2000

Sweetie,

Waking each day, only to realize you are not with me, is the cruelest torture. I miss your soft voice, your eyes, and the tender touch of your hands. Memories of you and your gentle loving heart, of us, of the children and grandchildren, stir me from dreams, occupying my every waking moment. Each day's passing is hollow time wasted without you, my intimate companion, my conscience, the defining grace of my ego. My spiritual pursuit of you continues through endless introductions and interactions with others, stumbling through the cold irony of life. I know from the moment our journey of life begins, death is its inevitable end. The distressing mystery for each of us is simply how and when. I just can't help but wonder: If death is our only option, the one, simple conclusion to birth, then why do we obsess our whole lives with trivial philosophies concerning right and wrong, good and evil, always trying to make sense of it all, when it will never make sense? Have the gods, in a battle of unassuming wit, finally defeated my spirit? All I know is no fear I have ever felt is greater than my fear of being without you. I miss your voice, your touch. I love you, Lottie. I always have.

A startling high-pitched clanging of mechanical revelry shatters the silence. Lowering the pen, I place it exactly perpendicular to the journal, leave my perch at the desk, and shuffle over to the nightstand to switch off the alarm. Grabbing a small, black vinyl toiletries kit from my overnight bag, I head toward the door. Captivated by the sliver of light creeping in from beneath I pause a moment, hoping some shred of truth will reveal itself as I step into the light beyond. *Did she make the right decision? God, I wish I knew. I dread today and this trip.* A fluorescent glare floods the room as I open the door, step into the hallway, and make my way to the ship's communal bathroom for a shave and long, hot shower.

Staring into the mirror, I hardly recognize my own reflection. Who is this shell of a man with puffy eyes and not-so-subtle wrinkles? I want to blame it all on sleep deprivation, but I know it is only part of the reason. Time, my life, has been slipping away faster and faster every year. I feel it more now than ever before. My sense of day and time has become a blur. *God, has it already been a week?*

After generously applying shaving gel to help the razor glide gently over this uneven terrain, I methodically move the razor across my face: first left, then right, then down. Always the same pattern. As I step into the shower, steam fills the small room like a dense fog. I cannot help but dream of her. It is a simple dream. We are in our kitchen having breakfast: scrambled eggs and coffee for me, just coffee for her. We chat while I eat and she sips her coffee between yawns. I tease her about being a delightful morning person. She says: *'NOT!'* Then, she lets out a little giggle, and flashes me a coy smile as she pats my hand. I hear her laugh. I feel her touch. The vision is so real. It manifests itself within my conscience leaving me believing that when I return to my room she will be there: at the same time, knowing she will not. Since receiving the news, each day has begun with the same regimen, the same dream, the same disappointment, the same emptiness.

Back in my room, I systematically complete the usual daily preparations, double-checking to make sure I have not forgotten anything. All things in order, I grab my coat and make my way to the metal stairs leading topside to where the galley is located. As I open the door and step out onto the open deck, a brisk wind assails me, stinging my freshly shaven skin. It stiffens my still-wet hair making it very clear I should have grabbed my hat.

This is the final leg of a trip taking me from Charlotte, North Carolina, in the United States, to Liverpool, England, by air. Having missed my connecting flight in Liverpool, I boarded this ship bound for Douglas on the Isle of Man. Although the deck is bustling with passengers and staff going about their morning rituals and greeting each other with involuntary politeness, all I feel is numb and alone. I shiver, not so much from the chilly air as from the thought of my mission going forward. I know I need to be here. I need to find answers. I need to do this for her.

As the ship chugs headlong into choppy waters, rounds of undulating waves strike the hull creating sporadic gusts of spraying mist. I make my way along the promenade deck, using the outline of the wooden planks for a measure of my waning balance, maneuvering around twin funnels and billowing black smoke, past a long row of round windows. Finally, I reach the aft deck. A few of the other passengers have gathered under an awning near the outer entrance of the galley, attempting to shield themselves from undesirable elements. Surveying the strangers around me, I see several groups of three and four huddled together for warmth, each wrapped mostly in beige and black overcoats. The women are wearing faux fur pillboxes, knit bobbles, and wool berets to protect their hair from becoming a windblown mess, while the men cover their receding hairlines with fedoras and Pendleton's, trying to keep the cold at bay. Most of them look like mannequins, without expression, listing with each sway of the rocking deck. A larger group, further away, has formed a circle, creating a human smokestack. An interminable haze of gray billows out through the top, dispersing the distinct odor of cigarettes and maybe even a cigar or two.

One of the strangers, a man as tall as he is wide, is standing alone outside the circle of smokers, turning his body left and right as if trying to use his size to block the relentless southwest wind and light his pipe. He keeps grabbing his green and black checkered derby, in an effort to keep it on his head. Eventually, the brisk breeze wins the tug-o-war and the man finally concedes, securing the hat under his left arm. I cannot help but notice the lack of hair on top of his head is more than compensated for by an abundance of it on each side. His unkempt muttonchops of unevenly-blended shades of orange and gray are bridged by a darker, very thick, handlebar mustache.

I approach him sympathetically, wind to my side, thinking I will help block the breeze, supporting his vain efforts to spark a flame. Assuming he might be Irish, because of the derby and matching checkered jacket, I decide to greet him using one of three Irish words I presume mean 'hello.'

"Bloody hell," he says, stuffing his still cold pipe and useless lighter into his coat pocket. "Are you American? Over on holiday? Too early for the TT. Let's see, races are usually in June, aren't they?"

"Yes. I'm American," I answer. "And no, I'm not on holiday. You're not Irish?"

"Oh, no, no. I'm an Aussie. Land down under and all that. And I am on holiday. Well, a holiday of sorts. It's really an expedition of a personal nature. I'm Gil. Nice to meet you."

"Christian. Nice to meet you. A holiday of sorts, you say?"

"Right, yes. It's a bit of a homecoming actually."

"So, you're from the UK?"

"No. Well, not originally. I'm coming here to, um, well, hopefully, connect with someone I haven't seen in a long time."

"Oh, I see. You just sounded like, well . . ."

"I was here a lifetime ago. Just a young lad full of vigor, ready to make my mark. Oh well, that was then. Anyway, been a pensioner for a while now and I decided to travel the world. Already been to the Philippines, Indonesia, South Pacific, the States. Never forgot being here as a young man, though. Thought I'd like to see what it's like now. See if I run into anyone I used to know."

"Wow, that's a lot of traveling. You've sure got me beat."

"I love traveling, mostly for the adventure. It's also very educational, you know. Visiting new places. Meeting new people. Well and the women, you meet a lot of women. Yes, well I guess women could fall within the category of education as well. Right? Occasionally, I pick up odd jobs along the way too. Makes for interesting conversation later."

"I bet it does. So, you travel alone?"

"Right, yes. I'm not married. Not anymore. I was married for a while. It didn't work out. She was a homebody, that woman. Pretty woman, though not a very good wife. Loved her things mostly. Hated travel of any sort, as it turns out."

"As it turns out?"

"Well, when we met and were first dating, she seemed quite interested in traveling. After we married, over the years, she lost interest. Oh, she loved to shop: clothing, shoes, jewelry. Mostly jewelry. When I suggested we travel the seven seas, you know, when I became a pensioner, she said she had developed a fear of water, become phobic or some such thing. So, I offered to fly her to the destinations.

I said we could meet when we arrived: her by air, me by sea. Well, she said she couldn't stand flying either. Said traveling in cramped quarters was like being stuffed into a petri dish of germs. The other passengers would be sneezing and coughing all over her. I tried to understand it; but then, she wanted me to stay put as well. I told her life is too short and I wanted to see the world. I didn't want to spend the last of my years living a mediocre life. I want to live, not just exist. All those years talking about seeing the world and it seems all she really wanted to do was sit. Well, and shop."

"That must've been difficult. I mean, to attach yourself to someone you think is your soul mate, make plans for the future, share hopes and dreams, only to discover your relationship is nothing more than unrequited love."

"Oh no. Quite the contrary. That was the problem from the start. She was never my soul mate. It seemed we were always going in opposite directions. I guess in the beginning we tried. You know we both enjoyed companionship. In the end, we were just too different. So, she chose to stay and I chose to leave. No hard feelings. Simple as that. Soul mate. Ridiculous concept. Silly really."

There is a long pause in our conversation, as we both gaze out past the ship's railing at distant patches of emerald, magically peeking between plumes of gray, appearing to float on the edge of the horizon. Gentle, rolling hills all different shades of jade are dotted with dancing shadows created by black-bottomed cumulus clouds skittering intermittently overhead. In this moment, I think the isle is a mystical thing, carefree, like a bird with its enormous wings spread out across the vast sea.

A blast of frigid air encourages us to move our conversation out of the moist cold into the warm, dry shelter of the galley bar. Dark maple paneling wraps around the bottom of each wall of the open room. Scattered across the top half are frames filled with old newspaper clippings and handmade posters of humorous quotes from notable individuals. They are all deliberately placed, creating a unique pattern of orderliness on the eggshell painted surface. The glow from a few brass lighting fixtures scattered around gives a sense of cordiality and warmth. At the near end of the room is a bar made of dark walnut stained wood, coated in several layers of polyurethane creating a murky, dull sheen. It is well-worn with stains, dents, carved initials, and etchings left by prior travelers. Matching heavy wooden tables, with two or three chairs each, fill the small dining space. The chairs rock gently with each slight pitch of the sea, slowly creeping away from their assigned spot. Glasses and bottles chime rhythmically with each rocking motion giving the illusion they are a band of tiny crystal musicians, and the chairs are dancers swaying to the tune they play. As I inhale, my appetite is stirred by the sweet aroma of caramelized onions and sausages emanating from the kitchen.

Gil and I seat ourselves at one of the small tables, beside a round, fingerprint-smeared window. He removes his overcoat, unbuttons his vest, and pulls a handkerchief from his breast pocket, wiping his mouth as he turns to look at the bartender. The bartender is preoccupied, busy replenishing salt and pepper shakers and napkin dispensers. He is a burly fellow, tall, with an abnormally large upper torso. He reminds me of a professional wrestler and looks like he could hold his own in a scuffle. He has kind eyes and an engaging, crooked smile which seem contradictory of his daunting physique. Gil hails him with his handkerchief. The bartender says he serves lagers and stouts later in the day, but assures us he can 'throw together' a Bloody Mary any time. We put in an order for two, extra spicy. I notice we are mostly alone in this shelter away from the harsh elements as I remove my coat and place it on a chair beside me.

"So ... are you a married man?" Gil asks.

"Yes I am. A long time. We married very young by today's standard."

"You said you are American."

"Yes. Born in Minnesota. Lived and worked in various places around the country. Military for a while, then corporate. Now I work for the government. I'll retire in a few more years."

"Right, yes. Well what brings you here then: business or pleasure?"

"I've come ... uh ... well ..."

"Oh, I apologize. I shouldn't be so nosey. Seems this may not be such an easy question to answer."

"No. It's okay. I, uh, I'm on my way to pick up some of my wife's belongings."

"I see. I'm sorry. The way you speak makes it sound unpleasant."

"Well . . . I mean, you see, she had been here on a dig."

"A dig? Oh, an archaeologist? How interesting. You sound sort of past tense though."

"Well, not an archaeologist. She's an artist. She was asked to do some sketches for an archaeological team on the Island. They were going to put her drawings in a future publication, but . . ."

Just then, a few passengers burst through the door complaining about the frigid air and the mist now turning to a light drizzle. This causes just enough commotion for me to redirect Gil's current line of questioning.

As a maneuver to reverse his innocent inquisition I say,

"Tell me about this trip of yours."

He sits forward in his chair, excited to engage. "Well, Christian, I finally have no responsibilities, no obligations. No, now it's just me. Like I said, I always wanted to travel, so now I am."

The bartender delivers to us what look to be very fortifying Bloody Marys. I pay the tab for both as Gil hoists his glass, giving an oddly solemn toast.

"To two lonely travelers." He stares at his glass as if recalling a distant memory. Following a slow sip through the long, black straw, he reposes. "Right, yes. You know . . . this notion of yours, Christian, that people can be soul mates, borders on ludicrous. There may be a perfect person for each of us out there. I just think finding them in the first place would be impossible. And holding on to them, well, it's ridiculous to believe that could happen, especially in this day and age."

"Don't misunderstand, Gil. Sure, some people think when you find your soul mate you hear harps playing and see shooting stars when you kiss; however, I believe finding your soul mate is different. It's a choice you make. You know, once you find someone you love being with, want to share your life with and decide to commit to, your partner becomes your soul mate. They're someone to share your true inner-self with, someone to trust with your darkest secrets, your greatest fears and your wildest dreams."

"Oh please, you're too sappy. It didn't work that way for me. I tried . . . at least I like to think I did. Anyway, I'm done. I'm moving on with my life. You do know marriage is merely a civil agreement: a contract. It's not love. Bloody hell man, half the marriages end in divorce nowadays anyway you know. Sorry to suck the romance out of it."

"Well personally, I have to disagree with you, Gil. I know life isn't easy, but if spouses, partners, work together taking on all the crap life throws at them, I think it makes them stronger, together, more of a team. For me, marriage is important, significant. It's a tradition I chose to hold on to. I realize in today's society long-term marriages are becoming a thing of the past. I agree with you there. And, sure, I agree there are legitimate circumstances where breaking up with your partner may be the right choice. It's just the way things are now, it seems like no one even tries anymore. As soon as it gets tough they give up. I'm not saying that's what you did. I just, well . . ."

"Right, yes. Well, I believe we should all be free to make our own choices in life. I made mine and I feel good about it. It might not be right for you, but it was right for me. Sometimes, when a situation can't be resolved, you need to choose to accept it and move on for your own sanity's sake."

Gil takes another long sip and his demeanor suddenly shifts. He lets out a slow sigh, leans back in his chair, slouching his shoulders. He abandons his bold rhetoric, revealing feelings obscured by his boisterous façade.

"You know I'm not a complete cynic. I'm not without heart. I loved a woman once and when I think of her, I still ask myself: What if it had been different?"

"Different?"

"Right, yes. Well it was a long time ago. Long before I was married to my, well, my recent ex."

"First love? Youthful sweetheart?"

"We were engaged to be married actually. It was the right thing to do, given our situation. You see, she and I had become quite amorous one spring, and, well one thing led to another. I was a free-spirited college freshman and she was a randy little high school junior."

"Engaged?"

"Well, as it turns out, she wasn't ready for that commitment."

"So, you didn't make it to the altar?"

"No. God no. She left me that winter. Dropped out of school and chose to raise our child on her own. I think she was trying to protect me, somehow. Her name was Mary. What a beautiful smile she had too."

"So, you still think of her? Mary?"

"Well, yes, I do, from time to time. My Mary. I wonder about our child and how they've lived all these years. I used to send letters to an old address, but they were always returned unopened."

"Sounds like you still miss her."

"Yes. Sometimes, especially as I get older, I think what if circumstances would have been different? What if one slight change could have caused the story to end another way?"

"Well I . . . "

"No, I know you can't see, can you? Because your life turned out well. You lucked out, so to say, finding your soul mate first off."

"I was lucky, Gil. I can't disagree."

"You can't possibly understand. I know I come across as cynical. I always have. Now I'm old, and tired. I've crossed over. I'm on the downward side of the hill. The story of my life may be ending soon. Still, I ask myself, what if the woman I loved actually loved me and we could be together? I mean, what if she left because she was afraid? Not thinking soundly at the time? What if . . . well, what if I had begged her to stay? What if she . . . "

"Come on, what makes you think your story is coming to an end? What if there is a new chapter yet to be written?"

His melancholy mood throws me off, so I awkwardly pick the celery stalk out of my Bloody Mary and take a bite. The crispness makes a snapping sound, which seems to act like a hypnotist's fingers and he at once regains his boisterous composure.

"Right, yes. Of course. Well, Mister Christian, I do believe, in the end, when the story is told, there will be another chapter to my life. Maybe I will find the woman of my dreams here on this lovely island. One can hope, right?"

He and I chuckle and he makes another toast.

"To two lonely travelers. One, lucky in love: the other, still hoping."

We continue to gaze around the room and out the window, finishing our drinks in silence. After a few moments, I sense my attention waning.

"Well, Gil," I offer as I push back my chair, "I wish you the best of luck." It is a clear and distinctive signal I have sent, suggesting this session of nostalgia, philosophy, and confession has come to a conclusion. We both stand. Gil slips on his coat, places his hat under his arm and prepares to exit the warmth of this shelter.

"It has been very nice to meet you, Christian. Thanks for the chat. Maybe I'll see you again sometime."

"It's very possible. Good luck with your next chapter, Gil."

We grip hands, shaking vigorously in agreement. Gil exits with haste as I retrieve my coat from the chair and prepare to leave.

Just then, a loud crash is heard coming from the kitchen. It is followed by a voice in great despair, bursting out at first, then tapering to a whimper. Already on my feet, and in close proximity, I dash in the direction of the noise. Two men sitting nearby jump from their chairs.

Another man slides out from his stool at the bar. Together, they fall in behind me rushing toward the galley doors behind the bar. I am first to enter the small kitchen, packed tightly with cluttered shelves and countertops, with only a small walkway to maneuver around a center table. The strong odor of fresh cut onion and minced garlic is overwhelming, stinging my eyes and burning my nose. Looking around the room, I see the stovetop crowded with a stockpot of potatoes bubbling in murky water, a frying pan filled with cocked sausages, and another pan full of sautéed vegetables, each emitting their own individual smells. At the far end of a long stainless-steel table, occupying much of the center of the room, past small storage containers, wraps and foils, I see a large cutting knife lying on its side. Its long, steel blade is blanketed in a pool of dark red fluid. More red flows across the tabletop trickling off the edge and culminating in a puddle of crimson on the shiny white tiles of the galley floor.

There, on the floor, is an old man slumped against one of the cabinet doors, holding a makeshift handkerchief bandage draped over an obvious wound to his left hand. Another man, dressed in all white, wearing a round paper cap, and food-stained apron, is kneeling beside him. He looks at me with a desperate expression of fear and disbelief as he struggles to comfort the old man. I turn to the men who have followed me into the galley and tell them it looks like everything is under control. Speaking in chatty whispers they try to peer over my shoulder around the tiny room. Suggesting they disperse, the men reluctantly turn and walk away one-by-one. When they are gone, I address the man in the apron.

"Are you in charge? Is there anything I can do to assist?"

"It's not as bad as it looks," he says. "The old man's a little beside himself, that's all. Small slice. Not too deep."

I frown and move in to assess the bandaged hand. There is no resistance to my actions as I kneel, placing my hands around the bloodied cloth. The man in the apron and I trade places without speaking. As he stands, I see he is of a solid build with heavily tattooed arms revealing a history of exotic destinations and endless stories. His white cap sits loosely on his clean-shaven scalp. Crystal blue eyes sink deep under thick, black brows which match his goatee.

"More injury to this man's pride than anything. You'll be okay, you old bugger," he barks at the old man. "Don't belong here anyway." He steps out a back entry into the service hallway where I hear him pick up the ship's telephone and call for assistance.

"What happened?" I ask the old man.

He is slow to respond. His skeletal face and hollowed eyes are etched with humiliation and anger, as well as pain. The whites of his eyes appear yellowed, fractured by small red blood vessels. His hands, with their blue bulging veins, freckled leathery skin and swollen knuckles, reveal signs of a long, hard life. He shifts his glance away from me.

With Cook out of the room, it is just the two of us: me an outsider from a faraway land, here completely by circumstance, him, a cocky, tough old veteran who presently finds himself in an awkward moment of dependency.

"I may be old, but I'm not stupid. I know better. I remembered to use my sea legs to balance."

"Never mind your legs. It's your hand I'm worried about."

"I just lost my focus for a moment, dammit."

"Don't worry. I'm sure you'll be fine."

"I'm not worried. And don't you feel sorry for me, either. I'm as capable as any man half my age. It's not like I'm some useless old man who's nothing but a bundle of problems and service needs."

"Sure. I understand. You're a war veteran, aren't you?"

"Yes, and damn proud of it."

"I am very aware of the contributions, the achievements, of your generation. Men like you are the original article."

"Well you're either full of shit, or you're a rare one for sure. It's been my experience the younger generation sees mine as outdated relics, useless to them in their pursuit of progress. Seems society is infatuated by youth and constant change, making my generation feel we are nothing but a drain on society: on everybody."

"Not me. I don't think anything like that. I truly respect men of your age."

"Cook said he would take it, take the meat, my meat, and chop it up and throw it in with the eggs so the other men could have some. I told him it was mine. Son-of-a-bitch."

For a moment, I sense I am in the presence of a proud bird, a falcon, the European raptor, captured in the wild to live out the rest of his years in a tight little cage, at the mercy and whims of his keeper.

Cook returns from the back hallway.

"How's the old man?" he asks, looking directly at me.

I glare back at him, cocking one eyebrow sarcastically. "Better—*now*." I answer, glancing at my new mate.

"Well, Captain wants him back in his own cabin as soon as possible. The medic will take a look at him before we go ashore." His monotone speaking reveals he has no clear feeling or understanding how his words, his actions, offended the old man.

"I'll see him to his room," I volunteer.

"Fine, I'm busy anyway."

We stand together, the old man and me, and exit through the service doorway, which leads below to the crew's quarters. We work off each other's balance as we descend the stairs and navigate the narrow corridor, crossing in tandem through a bulkhead doorway. About the time we get to his room, one of the ship's crewmen approaches us, and watches as I assist the old man into his quarters.

"Captain would like to see you, sir."

"Me?"

"Just you, sir. I will escort you, when you are ready, sir."

With the old man settled in a chair waiting for the medic to arrive, I follow the seaman along a steel walkway crowded with riveted metal beams and rust-colored pipes, which randomly burst wisps of steam. Small glass lamps, wrapped in metal cages and hung with enough wire to allow them to swing with the rocking ship, line the passageway. Along the route I notice the shuffling impatience of the crew, weary from a long night on duty and eager for relief. The odor of cleaning chemicals and freshly laundered bedding fills this small walkway in the underbelly of the ship. We pass a couple of young sailors with intense expressions on their faces, frantically scribing notes into their journals, capturing every detail of random information dictated to them by older, more experienced, crewmen. I feel out of place, like I am participating in a play and everyone has the script except me.

Following my guide, we turn at the end of this narrow passageway and enter a space three times as wide. An ornately trimmed floor runner, with a dark green field framed by golden leaves woven into a French blue border, flows over a polished hardwood floor. Warm complementary hues layer the top half of the walls, while the bottom half of each is adorned with grooved, vertical walnut paneling. Large walnut stained doors with engraved brass nameplates are evenly spaced on each side of the passageway. Lighting fixtures with candle-shaped bulbs and white linen shades illuminate the path.

Nearing the end of this lavish passageway, my escort abruptly stops. The sign on the door in front of us says only one word: Captain. Unaware of why I have been summoned, paranoia rapidly overtakes me. I feel like I have been kidnapped; marched to meet my captor. Heart pounding, I wonder what a real ship's captain is like? The only ones I had ever seen were in the movies. Ahab? Nemo? Bligh? I knew by context this one man was lord of his domain, demanding respect from his crew and all those who sail with him. *What kind of daunting figure awaits me?*

The crewman opens the solid wooden door. As I step into the dimly lit chamber, I detect the thick fragrance of amaretto-scented tobacco smoke lingering in the air. In contrast to my cabin, and the old man's, this room is grand and immaculately decorated. An arching brass lamp illuminates the surface of a large mahogany desk covered in charts, maps, and small measuring instruments. A chestnut-brown leather chair fits comfortably between the desk and floor-to-ceiling, built-in bookcases matching the desk. Several fencing trophies are displayed intermittently between volumes of hardbound books. A pair of mounted sabers, crisscrossed over a wooden shield, hang on the wall directly behind the desk between the towering bookcases. On the opposite side of the room, two winged-back leather chairs flank a small table containing a radio, an ashtray, two empty glasses and a full bottle of Jameson. In the background, I can faintly hear the haunting melody of 'Charade' playing on the radio, its sad lyrics mourning a lost love.

Seated in one of the chairs is a thin, distinguished-looking man. He is well-dressed in a tailored, dark blue jacket with gold buttons, perfectly pressed white pants, and well-polished wingtip shoes. He rises upon my entry and crosses the room to greet me.

"Welcome, my friend," he speaks in a strong, confident

voice. "I am Captain Aiza, Captain Antton Aiza. And you are?" His words trail off, prompting my reply.

To my surprise, he is not at all what I had feared. Rather, it seems he is less of a giant: a mere mortal after all. His mannerisms give the impression he is a well-educated man and of a high station within society. My pause is unintentional and must seem to take a very long time.

"Christian," I finally answer.

"Ah, Christian. A fine surname, albeit a rather common one, given our destination." He begins to pace a few steps back and forth as he continues. "The old man you cared for just now . . . "

"In the galley?"

"Yes. He is my father."

"Your father? Oh, I didn't know."

"No. Of course not. He stays with me now. I care for his well-being. He depends on me, although, if you ask him, he will deny it. He is old and has a weak heart, however, he is very strong-willed and would never admit he needs anyone. Too proud I guess."

"I understand. I sensed that when we were talking."

"Are you traveling for business, Mister Christian?"

"No."

"Ah, then for pleasure?"

"Well, no."

"Oh, I see. A man who travels for neither business nor pleasure. Makes it sound like you are a man of mystery." He glances at the bottle of Jameson and gestures to me.

"May I offer you a drink?"

"Yes, thank you."

He opens the bottle and pours a little less than two fingers into each glass.

"A toast to you, my friend," he says, handing me the drink. "A man of mystery. A man of clear compassion. And also, I think, a man of character. I sense a measurable level of sophistication in you, not unlike myself."

We raise our glasses and take a sip. The whiskey is pleasantly smooth in my mouth. As I swallow, I feel the familiar warmth of this caramel-colored liquid flow down my esophagus, radiating into my chest.

"I had forgotten how smooth Jameson is," I say as we both take another sip.

"You are a married man, Christian?"

"Well, yes, actually."

"Married a long time?"

"Yes. And you?"

"Me? No. Not anymore. After my wife passed away a few years ago. I realized my soul is betrothed to the sea."

"The sea?"

"She is one woman I will never lose. I find her soothing, intriguing. With her, I am most content."

"So, the sea is more than your profession. It's your passion: your love?"

"Well put, my friend. The sea is my passion. I respect her. I depend on her for my livelihood. I cannot imagine my life away from her. Although, she can turn rapidly and be as dangerous as any woman. Ah . . . women, love, life. It is all very strange . . . very strange indeed. Just when you think you have it all figured out, when you are comfortably numb in your routine, life throws you a curve ball. Quickly, you find yourself grasping to hold on to anything normal. For me that is the sea."

Taking another sip of whiskey, he places his nearly empty glass on the table and moves to a corner of the room further away from me. Then, in an oddly contemplative tone, he continues.

"You know something, Christian? I am the bastard son of a bastard. My father, the frail old man you just helped, left my mother at the birthing table minutes after I was born. He told her he would return some day as a decent and respectable man, a man she could be proud of, a man with money: except he never did. My poor mother worked all day, every day, to pay rent, bills, buy food and make sure I had clothes to wear.

"From an early age, I knew we were less fortunate than other families. The other children would go home after school to spend the evening with their parents and siblings, do their homework, enjoy dinner and family conversation. I remember gazing through their windows, watching how they were, always wishing I could have that kind of life.

"But, my reality consisted of a mother I hardly knew waking me early, telling me to eat breakfast and reminding me to take my sack lunch to school. She usually had to work late and would not be home for dinner, so I would eat without her and go to bed on time. Every morning, she handed me a key to our flat and walked out the door without looking back. Late in the evening, she would return, prepare my lunch and dinner for the next day, go to bed and start the whole routine again.

"My classmates were always taunting me, reminding me of my low station in life, saying awful things about my mother. They loved to make me angry. Over time, a rage built up inside me. I hated my life, my father, even my mother. I was lucky, Christian. My school teachers knew the life I lived. I am certain that is why they were extra kind to me. They helped me see things differently, helped me realize my potential. Because of them, and other compassionate souls I met as I grew older, I resolved to prove my strength. I would overcome the endless assaults and thoughtless malice of my schoolmates, not with anger or aggression, but instead with self-control and patience. I was determined to be stronger than the anger inside me.

"My mother never told me who my father was until a few years ago when she knew she was dying. I decided I wanted to meet him, confront him, tell him how he had ruined our lives. So, I tracked him to a halfway house in Lisbon. It was a horrible place. I told him who I was and asked him why he never came back. He said he always planned to, except he never made anything of himself. He had enlisted in the army for a while. When he got out he just could not cope. Demons, I guess. Anyway, after that he was too ashamed to find us. He thought we would be better off without him. I am not sure why, but in that moment, when he had told me everything, the reasons behind his choice to stay away, all I could see was a frail old man with little time left to regret the sins of his past. In that single moment, all the anger I had for him all those years vanished. I could not leave him in that wretched place, so I brought him here to live with me."

"He left you, and your mother, and never tried to find you. You were subjected to ridicule all during your childhood for not being like everyone else, for not having a 'normal' life. I don't understand how you could be so forgiving, so generous, to someone who caused you so much pain."

"Well, Christian, over the years, I have learned you must accept people for who they are, not for what you want, or wanted, them to be. Even though he was not a good father to me, he was a father figure to others. He fought many battles during his time in the service, battles for the good of the country: for mankind. It is not for me to judge him for what he was not, or what he did not do. Rather, I choose to recognize his contributions to society overall.

"When my mother finally told me about him she said that, back when they first met, my father led a small pack of self-proclaimed *Miqueletes* near Gipuzkoa. The Miqueletes, you see, were skirmishers who harassed street gangs to keep them from bothering good citizens. He was, to the Miqueletes, what a father represents to his family. The people there called it 'Fides'—the faith. The Miqueletes respected him. They loved him. And so, they called my father Fides, the faith of his household. I do not expect you to understand why I took him in after all this time. It is just something I chose to do. I am caring for a dying old man for no other reason except that he is my father. I do not condone some of his choices in life. Trust me, I wish he would have been around while I was growing up. I guess, in a way, I am being selfish. It benefits me more than it does him. It makes me feel like a better person, compassionate, not just an indifferent old ship's captain."

"So, forgiving your father, your generosity toward him, helps you heal, overcome your anger, gives you a chance to connect. I think I understand."

"Yes, Christian, caring for my father is a way for me to do that. I spent a lifetime defending myself against senseless, hurtful, acts of others and do you know what I have learned, Christian? I have learned the power of forgiveness is greater than any act of anger or revenge. I believe the true path to personal happiness, to self-actualization, is to learn empathy. To show compassion and generosity instead of judgement and condemnation. By choosing to show my father sympathy now, I control all the anger I felt as a child, instead of the other way around. Yes. Power to overcome pain and suffering, I think that is my strength. I only share all this with you because I sense much good in you, also, a deep sadness. Well, enough of this," he says walking toward the desk, pointing at an old book on one of the high shelves. "You have heard of John Donne?"

"English poet, right?"

"Yes, Christian. Very good."

"He's famous for writing, 'No man is an island entire of itself. Every man is a piece of the continent; part of the main.' Something like that?"

"Yes, that is right."

"I know his work pretty well. However, I don't necessarily accept his theory. No, in fact, contrary to what Donne wrote so long ago, I believe each man is an isle unto himself, entire of himself. Completely whole."

"Ah . . . your theory suggests man is more like the Fortunate Isles of mythology. Blessed with abundance. Self-reliant. I think Donne was saying human beings cannot thrive, cannot exist, when isolated from others. I believe his real meaning lies clearly at the end of the phrase, where he says we are part of the main."

"Well . . . maybe it's because of my childhood . . . the way I was raised. I was a latch-key kid, not unlike you. Even though I had both my parents and four siblings, we were all disconnected—dysfunctional as a family unit. From the time I was eight years old, my mother and father both worked long hours. My siblings and I had to fend for ourselves. I was much younger than the rest of them, the unexpected result of failed birth control. My brothers and sisters would go to school before me and come home after, so I was alone most of the time. I had to become self-sufficient: make my own breakfast, remember my house key. I've been that way my whole life."

"I see what you are saying, however, you must agree it is better to be part of a group, helping and supporting each other, rather than trying to isolate ourselves. You said you are a married man. I would think you need and rely on your wife?"

"Captain, please don't get me wrong, I dearly love my wife, and my family. I would do anything to help them, to protect them. That has nothing to do with it. I see it like this: The world is full of many diverse people grouped together by fate, creating larger communities, but do they need each other to survive? I don't think so. I coexist with those around me. I accept all the social requirements of living in society. I'm actually very kind and compassionate by nature, yet I don't rely on others to tell me what to do or how to think. No, I make my own choices. I don't need the acceptance of anyone else to give me self-worth. In that respect, I feel I am an island unto myself . . . an isle of man, if you will."

"Please do not take offense, however, that seems a contradiction to me. A compassionate soul who does not need anyone else. You are indeed very complex in your thinking, Mister Christian."

"Could be I just listened to Simon and Garfunkel too much as a kid . . . you know the lyrics 'I am a rock, I am an island.'"

There is a knock on the door.

"Enter," Captain Aiza barks.

"It's safe harbor ahead, sir," the crewman reports. "We're about thirty minutes out of Douglas, sir."

"Okay, tell the pilot I am coming top side," the captain replies.

As the crewmember leaves, the captain retrieves his glass from the table and empties the remaining whiskey with one swallow.

"Where are you lodging, Christian?"

"The Harbor House Inn, on the promenade."

"Good, we are staying just a block or so away from there at the Chesterhouse Hotel. I have stayed their many times. I find the accommodations quite comfortable, as well as very convenient. Join the old man and me for a drink before dinner?"

"Sure," I agree, as we place our empty glasses on the table. I turn toward the door, then stop. "Where should we meet?"

"A pub called 'Maggie's.' You cannot miss it. It is on the ground floor of your hotel. We will meet you there."

We shake hands and I follow him out. He disappears left to the forward deck. I turn right, making my way along the elegant passageway, back to the narrow, metal corridor leading to my cabin.

On the way to my room, I meet Cook still dressed as before, minus the cap and food-stained apron. He has been assigned to aid the old man with packing his things to go ashore. Something compels me to ask if he is interested in a drink later.

"Sure," he says. "Where?"

"A place called 'Maggie's.' It's on the first floor of the Harbor House Inn."

"I know the place, real good pub. I usually stop at 'Quids' though: more my style. Well, guess I better get the old man sorted out," he says, continuing down the hall.

Chapter Two

On deck, the same nameless strangers from earlier in the morning are huddled around as before. Nervous chattering swirls in the crisp air as the drizzle continues to increase. All are anxious to step on solid ground again. We watch as the vessel approaches the shoreline. Faced with the reality of this moment and what I must do here, a deep anxiety swells within in me. Observing this island in the middle of this vast sea, I cannot help but feel, like me, it stands very much alone.

God, all I ever wanted was to be a normal guy living a normal life! I think about the young man I once was, full of energy, passionate about life and adventures I would have. I remember the day I met a beautiful young girl, and later, when I asked her to be my wife, the happiness I felt when she agreed. Memories of places we lived, the birth of each of our baby girls, traveling the world together, sharing joy with our daughters when they found good men and married them, seeing a part of our life extend through the treasure of grandchildren: so many wonderful adventures, more than we ever expected. All these thoughts flash through my mind, propelling me through time to the day everything changed. Our world ambushed by an ugly monster. Now, here I stand, alone, in the middle of a crowd, feeling anything but normal.

Looking across the shore, I see mountain piled upon mountain, extending in a lofty range for many miles, in the center of which a larger peak rises with such grandeur, proudly claiming superiority. The rugged coastline to the south, overhung with glaring cliffs and crags, catches my eye. Even from a distance it seems to threaten the unwelcome voyager.

Steadier rain greets us offshore and escorts us into port. Entering the harbor, we pass what looks like a small castle with four thin turrets perched on the surface of a tiny knoll jutting out in the middle of the bay. I recall hearing one of the passengers say it connects to the mainland by an isthmus no wider than a walkway, revealed during only the lowest of tides.

The ship's horn blasts, announcing our arrival. It takes a while to dock the ship and disembark, but I am finally on land again and the feeling of constant swaying has stopped. I only have two bags: one is smaller and holds my journal, the other is a larger overnight bag. It would be easy to manage both in mild weather, but the winds have increased and the rain is steady, so I arrange with the porter for them to be delivered to my hotel. Taking my bags, he informs me the location of my accommodations is a mere ten-minute walk from here, a few hundred meters straight ahead along the promenade.

Lightly colored Victorian buildings, facing the harbor, line the wide promenade, containing eateries, small hotels, and business offices. The pattern of stoops ascending to double doors beside large bay windows repeats itself along the building fronts, from the beginning of each block to the end. Wrought iron gates and railing, designed to keep pedestrians from falling in, enclose small moats found in front of each casement. The classical architecture is interrupted only once by the insertion of a postmodern Protestant church wedged on a street corner. After this oddity, the historic pattern returns, continuing a few more blocks.

On the opposite side of the street a hardy workhorse, pulling a tram, dutifully plods forward, unfazed by the wind and rain. The driver is bundled warmly in a woolen coat with a scarf wrapped snugly around his head and face. The tram, which is empty now, has a basic frame with no walls and only a thin metal roof. Inside are bench seats in rows designed for tourists and exhausted pedestrians to board easily and have a great panoramic view of the shoreline.

Across the promenade, beyond a cemented walkway, lies a shoreline layered in places with large rocks, and snags of sea debris. The shoreline is dotted with dedicated beach casters braving this nasty weather in hopes of a good catch.

A street vendor on the next block closes the service window of his small cart and lowers the canopy to keep it from being battered by the unrelenting wind. Grasping the brim of my hat firmly, I tip my head to shield against the gusts. I straighten my coat collar and snug it tightly around my neck to keep the rain from seeping in and dampening my clothes. *Thankfully, I arranged for my bags to be delivered to the hotel instead of struggling with them in these adverse conditions.*

A few more steps and I find myself in front of a large elegant-looking building with ornately trimmed balconies on the upper levels. An engraved sign above the front door indicates I have arrived at my destination. Neon lights publicizing 'Maggie's Pub' illuminate a large bay window in the front corner of the building. As I enter this inviting space, it is clear the time for eating lunch has passed. The lounge area is empty except for a waitress busily cleaning off an eclectic collection of tables. Crossing to the dimly lit bar, I am greeted with a single upward nod by a young woman wearing a white shirt with long sleeves rolled up halfway, her right forearm exposing a colorful tattoo. Her red hair is cut short, and shaved high around her ear on one side. She stands upright, with shoulders back, vigorously cleaning a glass with a stark white bar towel.

"Afternoon," she says with a hint of an accent. "Name's Maggie. What can I get you?"

"Can I get a beer please?"

"Aye," she says as she places the glass she is holding carefully in a row with others and tosses the towel over her shoulder. "What's your strength? We've got six on tap from Beck's to Guinness."

Assessing the different labels on the handles attached to a brass t-shaped stanchion at the bar's center, I say, "I'll have a Stella."

She pours the drink into a tankard and carefully sets it on the counter in front of me, foam flowing over the side and pooling around the base. She returns to wiping another glass. Behind her are several liquor bottles positioned upside down on smaller taps. A few have inverted labels so they can be easily read right side up in this situation. Below the counter, built-in coolers store canned beer, fruit juices, sodas, and small bottles of white wine.

I sip my Stella and continue to pan the inside of the room. Tall side-by-side bay windows wrap around the alley side of the room and across the front wall, allowing for a magnificent view of the promenade. Tucked into a corner, near the front door, sits a retro Wurlitzer jukebox. Painted on a wooden board above the door is an old Manx saying: '*Dy chooilley ghooinney er e hon hene, as Yee son ain ooilley.*' Below it the English translation: 'Every man for himself, and God for us all.' A small television, anchored to a shelf high on the far back wall, is broadcasting an international cable news program. A story about President Clinton meeting with Russian President Vladimir Putin to discuss a new missile defense program that has just ended. The announcer begins to ramble on with other headlines of the day, such as economic reform, corruption, and global warming. The news feels different on this side of the globe. I am not interested—I have other things on my mind. To the right of the TV, in the opposite back corner, is a cork dartboard with a slate chalkboard beside it, displaying initials and scores of those who played last. I scan the rest of the walls decorated with a variety of posters and old newspaper clippings like those in the ship's galley. As my focus returns to the wall behind the bar, I notice an old photo of a hefty young man and a very pregnant young girl displayed prominently on a high shelf. They look very happily in love. I lift my tankard and savor the flavor of the cold beer as it passes my lips and quenches my thirst. Maggie sees me looking at the faded old picture of the couple.

"It's my mum and dad. Another?" she asks as she glances in the direction of my still half-filled glass.

"Not just yet. Waiting for a friend." I look away, peering out the window, glad to be inside the warm, dry bar.

"I never met him," her words interrupt the silence, capturing my attention. She nods toward the same picture. "That's me," she says, pointing to the woman's round belly. "Mum never married. Said she never loved anyone else except him." She looks away from the photo and out the window. "Good rain this week. Spring rain strengthens the sea. Good for those fishermen out there. Good for the farmers too," she says still attending to her task. She finishes the last glass, reaches into the sink, and gives a hearty tug on the rubber stopper to drain the water. "You on holiday?"

As I am about to answer her question, a distinguished-looking middle-aged man clatters through the front door escorting in a burst of chilly, wet air. Maggie, indifferent to whether I answer her question or not, disappears through a doorway at the end of the bar leading into the kitchen. Methodically, the man removes his coat, hat and gloves then swiftly makes his way to my side.

"Are you Mister Christian?" he asks in a very refined and articulate voice. He hangs his wet coat on a hook attached to a post at the end of the bar before he sits. His question and precise mannerism has piqued my curiosity.

"Yes. I am."

"Oh good. The captain at the terminal . . . he said you might be here."

"Captain Aiza."

"Yes. He said you two planned to meet here for a drink before dinner."

"What can I do for you? Did the captain send you?"

"No, no . . . I have some information for you but not from the captain."

"I'm sorry. I don't mean to be rude. I don't understand. Who are you and how do you know me?"

"Mercher. Gowerr Mercher at your service." He extends his thin, cold, brittle hand in greeting. He smiles faintly, revealing a row of crooked, stained teeth. An oddly thin pencil mustache enhances his equally thin upper lip.

"I was asked to be your guide while you are here. Well, not exactly asked. I volunteered to be your point of contact. The university wanted someone to fetch you when your plane arrived. I was not aware of your change of plans. Thank goodness airports and seaports are all in close proximity on this rock. I am either late, or you are early. Nevertheless, I missed your arrival and I apologize. I am certainly glad I have found you."

Reappearing from the kitchen, Maggie places a small steaming dish in front of me. "I found you a leftover pie from lunch. It's not much, but it's still pretty fresh. I warmed it for you."

"Thank you." I unfold my napkin and lay it over one knee. My mouth waters as I breathe in the aroma of warm

Cheddar cheese and shallot wafting out from beneath a buttery, flaky, fennel seed crust. It strikes me, at this moment, I do not remember if I ate anything this morning or if my nourishment so far has only consisted of three courses of beverage: The Bloody Mary with Gil, a whiskey with the captain and of course this now room-temperature, half-finished Stella.

"As I said," the man continues, trying to regain my attention. "The university wanted to make sure you get checked in properly today so we can make the most of your time tomorrow. I want to take you—"

Just then, the front door flies open again. This time it is the captain and the old man bringing another burst of freezing air. They shake off the rain, and place their wet things on a coat rack by the door.

"Christian," the captain says, acknowledging me, as he and his father approach the bar. "And Mister Mercher," he says with an expression of curiosity.

Mercher nods stiffly in response.

"Welcome to Avalon, gents. What's your poison?" Maggie says, quite confident in the presence of this odd, diverse group of strangers.

"We'll have what he's having and put his drink on my tab," the captain replies.

"Got it!'

"And for you, Mercher?" the captain asks. "What is your fancy?"

"Oh, Chardonnay please," he says looking to Maggie.

"Add his drink to my bill as well."

"Will do!" She fills the first mug, reaches across the

bar placing it in front of the captain's father, then begins to pour the second.

Sensing the old man is staring at me, I look over at him.

"He wants to say, 'thank you.' He was pretty impressed with you this morning. Told me you are as good a man as they come," the captain tells me.

"Well, I'm honored you think so," I address the old man. "I really didn't do much."

The captain looks at me, but his words are directed to Mercher.

"Mister Christian tells me he is here, visiting our little Island, neither for business or pleasure. And so now, with you entering the story, sir, the mystery grows."

"I would say that is a fair assessment of the purpose of his visit," Mercher responds with a brief glance in my direction. "You see, our Mister Christian here has come to gather some of his wife's personal belongings. It would be a slight deviation of truth to call it business, since it is more personal than corporate in this case. On the other hand, his visit certainly cannot be described as pleasure, I am sure. I do not think it uncommon for someone in his situation to provide a stranger, such as yourself, limited information." Mercher looks at me. "I hope I am not speaking out of order here."

"No, it's fine," I say.

Maggie serves the captain his drink and then places a glass of wine in front of Mercher.

"A toast, gentlemen," says Captain Aiza as he raises his mug. "To successful ventures and rewarding revelations."

Then he offers " . . . And, Mister Christian, to the isle called Man."

I nod, confirming my understanding of the inferred double meaning.

"Miss, may we move this party to one of the tables?" the captain inquires.

"Sure. Anywhere is fine."

Relocating from our perches to a small table near the bar, I carry the plate holding the pie and fork in one hand and the Stella in the other. We settle into our new vantage point, able to face each other.

"To address your dilemma specifically, Captain," Mercher explains, "I must first point out I have been looking forward to meeting Mister Christian. I had the privilege of working with his dear wife, if only briefly, and must say I was quite consumed by her grace and charm, not to mention she was quite attractive. I do not wish to put words into his mouth. Though just from what she said, I think their relationship quite abnormal, almost a state of being. A relationship like theirs is like a pairing of two souls." He looks at me and asks, "Is that a fair assessment?"

Before I can answer, the old man pipes up. "Pairing of two souls . . . nonsense! In my day, the only thing that mattered was getting a good cook and housekeeper. If a man wasn't careful, and I knew plenty that weren't, it could turn out to be a life sentence of burned biscuits and chewy steak." He rolls his eyes, stares into his half-filled mug, and takes a long swig.

"Yes. Well then," Mercher tries to ignore the old man's

remark. "Now, more to the point of Mister Christian's journey." He looks at me. "Tell me if I have said too much my good man."

"Oh, no . . . it's okay," I assure him.

"Good," Mercher looks at the captain as he continues his narrative. "First, let me give you some context. Christian's wife, Lottie, had been on an archaeological dig at Saint John's this past year. The university invited her as guest pro bono after months of correspondence. It seems they were aware of, and appreciated, her works of art and wanted her to use her talents to draw various scenes of the excavation for a forthcoming collegiate publication. During her stay, she took a day tour of Peel Castle, on our west coast, to see ancient parish remains within the ruins and the tomb of Bishop Rutter that was recently excavated."

"Did I hear you mention Peel?" Maggie asks from behind the bar. "Oh, I'm sorry for interrupting. My family is from Peel. I used to work at the House of Manannan." She looks at me as she explains. "It's a tourist stop near the harbor, close to the castle ruins. I worked there before my mum and I bought this place."

"Join us?" the captain offers.

"Sure, thank you. I can't refuse an invitation from such a handsome group of men." She shrugs and points behind her with her thumb. "And I'm pretty sure my dear business partner won't mind either."

I see a face identical to that of the pregnant girl from the photograph, only older, peering through a small porthole in the kitchen door.

The captain reaches over to a nearby table and pulls a chair up for our curious new acquaintance.

Mercher continues. "So, as I was saying, while there, a woman approached Lottie and gave her an old book, claiming it to be some original ancient manuscript, and asked her to keep it safe. From what I understand, it might be a written account of a ballad called, '*Fin and Oshin*,' one of the most controversial stories in Manx history." Mercher takes a sip of wine as he continues. "The official version of this mysterious ballad refers to another great man whose name is Gorry. The two, Fin and Gorry, were rival heroes. Fin was a chief hero of Celtic legends. Gorry was a younger, handsome princely character. The story says one day, when Gorry declined an invitation from Fin to ride along with him and his hunting party, the young girls of the village devised a plan to torment him and embarrass him in front of all the townsfolk."

"Why would they do that?" Maggie stands, not waiting for the answer. "Let me know if you want another round. Looks like I'm needed in the kitchen."

Mercher watches as she walks away. "Anyway, as I was saying, people believe Gorry was the type of man who respected God through nature. He worshipped creation and all creatures. He would not, could not, hunt and kill just for sport."

"Sounds like a true God-fearing 'one with nature' kind of guy," the old man remarks.

"Makes sense that he declined the invitation to hunt," I acknowledge. "It kind of sounds like he was a bit of a loner too."

"Indeed," Mercher adds. His voice begins to intensify. "You see, it was said to be Fin's daughter and her maidens who caught Gorry resting. They tied his hair to the ground with rope, and set burning coals near his feet. As his feet began to get hot, he awoke. Struggling, he could not untie himself. So, there he is, trapped in front of the townsfolk, and embarrassed. An indignity had been done to him, to his pride. At this point, Gorry vows to avenge and burn all their homes. Fire for fire. Enraged, he frantically gathers burthens of gorse from the mountainside to make torches, which he carries back to the village to burn the homes."

Mercher pauses for a moment, slowly swirling the remaining wine around in his glass, spilling a little over the edge.

"Go on," says the captain, encouraging our storyteller.

Gulping the last of his wine, Mercher sets his empty glass on the table. "Well, when Fin and his men see the smoke billowing up from the village they returned as quickly as possible. When they discovered what Gorry had done, they were upset and confused. They were oblivious to what had caused him to commit this atrocity, and of course the young maidens did not want to come forward and be punished for their part. The villagers said Gorry had gone mad, even physically changed, becoming like the feared buggane." Mercher pauses, sitting back in his chair apparently finished with his dissertation.

"Is that it?" asks the old man. "That's the ending?"

"No, well . . ." Mercher leans forward. "That is just it . . . you see, that is wherein lies the controversy. For generations people have questioned and debated the ending to the ballad. What we do know is during the time the vicars were revising and translating scriptures into the Manx language, a bishop named Rutter became interested in writing down the ancient ballads as well. He transcribed several, including this one. In the late seventeen hundreds the Bishop's work was sent to Copenhagen and also deposited in the British Museum, together with four other ballads. Sometime later, a Reverend Moore published it in *The Manx Notebook*, and later, in his collection of Manx Ballads."

"So, the ballad written by Bishop Rutter became the official version?" asks the captain.

"Yes." Mercher's tone changes as he continues. "It has long been alleged by historians, Bishop Rutter liked to put his own spin on his poetry and other writings. Through the years, people have insisted he put a spin on this ballad as well. It is rumored there was another written version of the same story, kept in secret."

"So, there are two written versions?" I ask.

"Some think so. The official version of Bishop Rutter, and a secret one laid to rest with him in his tomb. The original version, they claim. However, I am quite certain Rutter's official version is the original, correct account of the ballad. There would be no reason to change the ending to such a story."

"How does Rutter's official version end?" asks the old man.

"Oh, well . . . when the men of the village returned from the hunting trip and saw the damage the fires had done, they gathered to hunt Gorry. When they finally caught him, they had him drawn and quartered," Mercher explains.

"Why would they do such a thing?" the old man asks. "That sounds too extreme. The ancient people of this Island would never have done that. Weren't they all farmers and fishermen? They wouldn't have carried out such a severe punishment!" He looks at the captain. "I can't believe that's how the original ballad would have ended."

"Remember, old man, ballads were meant to be mere allegories to teach consequence for action," the captain reminds him. "You have taken this too literally."

"But, the old man raises a good point," I say. Mercher looks at me sharply. I continue. "What if you discovered the two versions of the written ballad were different?"

"Did I hear you say there was another version?" Maggie asks, returning to our table. "Do you think the two ended differently?"

"It's possible," I say.

"Conspiracy theory?" she asks.

"Mutation over time. Revisionism?" I suggest.

Mercher scoffs. "Both greatly overrated and misunderstood theories."

"On the contrary," I say. "Revisionism is quite common. It's well-known, historically, whoever is in charge at the time, gets to tell their version of events as the truth."

I pause, not sure how much to share with this group of strangers I have only just met, still something compels me to continue. "Like Mister Mercher said: When she was here . . . when she was at Peel, my wife was given an old manuscript. As she described it to me in her letters and telephone calls, she believed it told this same story with an entirely different ending. Possibly a more exact version of the original ballad."

"Before the Bishop's revision?" asks the old man.

"Lottie thought so," I answer. "Throughout history most, if not all, ballads had a moral lesson to be conveyed. As the captain pointed out, there was a consequence to be considered. Lottie told me Bishop Rutter translated his version of the ballad at a time when Christianity's ideals were being written in the local language and spread throughout the isles. His account was about fearing the penalties of what was considered unacceptable social and moral behavior at the time. It could be possible the Bishop took advantage of the timing, writing these ballads just as scriptures were being translated, putting his own twist on them to promote his religious beliefs."

"So, Christian," Captain Aiza surmises, "if an older written version, assuming there is one, of this ancient ballad, chronicled a disparate outcome, a completely different moral lesson might be learned."

Abruptly, the pub door swings open. Two young men enter, struggling to close the door against the force of the wind. Once it is closed, they help each other remove overcoats, hats, and scarves. The old man and Mercher shiver as the cool air ushered in crosses the room to our table, interrupting our chain of scrutiny and discussion. I notice both young men have similar short haircuts, piercings in their ears and lips, and what seem to be, at least from this distance, matching tattoos at the base of their necks. I watch as they pull their barstools closer to each other and take a seat.

"Excuse me," Maggie says as she pulls back her chair and returns to the bar to attend them.

I finish the last bite of my pie, which has cooled and hardened, fold my napkin on top the plate, and finish my Stella.

"Yes," I say, looking directly at Mercher. "It is possible there are two versions and they could be significantly different . . . at least the outcome."

"Possible, however, not very probable, Mister Christian," Mercher replies. "Have you seen the manuscript for yourself?"

"Not yet, I am hoping to read it soon though. It should be with Lottie's things."

"Oh, I thought you had, perhaps already received it from someone when you arrived. I see I am incorrect."

Maggie has come back to our table to remove my empty plate and retrieve our empty glasses. She points a finger at me.

"You're Christian, right?"

"Yes."

"Well a man who calls himself Cook just telephoned to say he can't make it after all. Stopped off at Quids instead."

"Ah . . . Cook . . . now there's a conflicted soul," the old man says. "Grew up pretty rough, pretends to have a tough shell. Comes across as a brute most of the time. He's really okay once you break through the barrier, soft-hearted even; although, I'd never say that to his face."

"Why do you always stand up for him no matter what he does?" the captain asks. "What about today in the kitchen?"

"Hell, we both just lost our tempers for a moment, that's all," the old man says. "I shouldn't have become so angry. All he wanted to do was share the meat with the crew. I think I've gotten crotchety in my old age."

Is it possible the Captain got his sympathetic demeanor from his father, even though he didn't know him growing up? I wonder.

"Another round for you gentlemen?" Maggie asks, interrupting my train of thought.

"None for me," the old man and Mercher respond in unison.

"I think this will do it for me as well," I answer.

"Thank you, Maggie, but we really must finish up and leave to check in at our hotel," the captain replies. "Let me ask you this, Mister Mercher: What if details were changed during translation to make the story reflect the wishes of those in control, to evoke a certain response? If the facts were changed, the thinking skewed, the response to the outcome . . . the moral of the story if you will, would have altered later actions of mankind, would they not?"

"Exactly my point!" I inject.

Mercher seems uneasy with this logic, but is interrupted before he can refute it.

"He's right," says one of the young men at the bar. "Pardon my intrusion," he says as he approaches our table, "but, hearing your conversation, I couldn't resist. We're with the Methodist church, just a couple of blocks from here. I overheard what you were talking about, and I thought, well Psalm 42:1 is one of my favorite verses in the bible. It says, in the King James version, 'as the hart,' that's h-a-r-t, meaning deer, 'panteth after the water brooks, so panteth my soul after thee oh God.' Recently others, self-help groups, song writers, and addiction centers across the world, have revised it for their own purposes.

"They have changed it to, 'as a heart,' h-e-a-r-t, 'longs for flowing streams . . .' Sorry, a h-e-a-r-t doesn't long for flowing streams: but, a h-a-r-t does. So, these revisionists of the Bible verse have erased the real meaning: changed it forever, all to make it fit what they are selling. People who accept the phrase as they have rewritten it, adapt to a different meaning. It kind of makes you wonder how many other things we believe and accept are actually revisions of something else."

The captain looks at me. We are all stunned at the young man's insight.

"Sorry," he says, "I didn't mean to . . . "

The captain stands and reaches out his hand. "Well spoken, young man. You are very wise. That is exactly what we were discussing. Thank you for sharing."

The young man nods meekly and returns to his partner at the bar. His companion pats him gently on the shoulder, whispering something in his ear.

"Well, gentlemen, this certainly has been a thought-provoking conversation. Now, however, I am going to pay the tab and take the old man to get checked in at our hotel."

Maggie escorts him to the register. The old man shuffles uncomfortably in his chair, laboring to rise.

Mercher speaks to me as he stands. "Mister Christian, you should be receiving a photocopy of the manuscript soon from one of the dig team members. The original will have been routed through my office to be cataloged and archived by now."

The captain returns to our table to assist the old man to the door. "Storm is going to get stronger the next few hours before things die down. You gentlemen might want to get settled in for the evening."

I rise from my chair. "Captain, thank you for your hospitality."

"Oh, it is I who owe you gratitude for your act of kindness toward my father earlier."

"Yeah," the old man says, "I'm glad you were there to help me to my room. I'm sorry for upsetting everyone. It's frustrating getting old in body when your mind is still sharp. Not sure how much longer this old ticker will keep me going," he says patting the left side of his chest.

As the captain and the old man make their way toward the exit, the front door swings open. A lanky young man, followed by a woman with long auburn hair, tied in a ponytail, stumbles in, appearing as if the breeze blew them in haphazardly. The captain and the old man close the door behind them and head off toward their hotel. Adjusting her thick black-rimmed glasses, the woman spots Mercher and walks over to us.

"Mister Mercher. This is a surprise."

"Good to see you, Doctor. This is Mister Christian, Lottie's husband."

"Nice to meet you, Mister Christian. I'm Vikki Clemmings. Oh, and this is my driver, Elan. We were hoping to find you here."

"Vikki specializes in Mesolithic and Neolithic cultures of Britain and Ireland, with a particular focus on monuments and landscape."

"Thank you, Mercher. I see you've read the university brochure ... "

"She also has a broader interest in hunting and gathering populations, interpretive archaeology and stone tools, I believe."

" ... and I see you've also read my biography as well."

"Nice to meet you, Vikki," I say, extending my hand to greet her. Then to the young man, "Elan. Is that right?"

"Yes sir, I worked with Miss Lottie at the dig site."

"Oh, so you knew her as well?"

"Yes, she was one of a kind. A really sweet woman. I think it was a noble thing she did."

Vikki and Mercher look aghast, upset by his cryptic words.

"I loved her artwork," Vikki says, in a mildly exuberant tone, trying to dissipate the awkwardness. "I'd seen her work before and when I found out she was volunteering I could hardly believe it."

"I thought you might have come earlier to deliver the copy of the manuscript to Mr. Christian," Mercher says to Vikki.

"You know . . . she was different after she read it, Miss Lottie," Elan says as his eyes drift to the ground.

Maggie comes around from behind the bar. "Can I offer you folks anything?"

We all decline and she disappears into the kitchen.

As Vikki and Mercher discuss coordination for my visit, Elan pulls me aside, away from Mercher.

"Here you are," he says, as he gently removes items from a worn leather bag. "This is one of Miss Lottie's binders, just draft ideas she had written down. The one with all her final sketches is in her satchel at the dig site with the rest of her supplies."

He pulls a second item from the bag. It has tattered, yellowed sheets of parchment paper bound between a thick leather cover, tied together with some sort of twine.

"Miss Lottie wanted you to have this. She wanted you to read it. She said you would understand," he says, almost whispering. "It's not a copy, Mister Christian. I didn't copy it. I was supposed to, but I didn't. Miss Lottie wanted to make sure you had the original, complete version. If I had requested it to be copied, then it would have gone through a review process and been redacted. That's Mercher's department and well . . . he thinks I had it reviewed and copied and the original is on its way to his office. Please keep it safe . . . don't let it go missing."

"Thank you, Elan," I say. As Mercher approaches us I deliberately tuck the manuscript inside the binder so he cannot see it.

Mercher looks at me. "I will come by tomorrow morning to retrieve you and escort you to the dig site so you can collect Lottie's things."

"Thank you, Mercher."

"Oh, Mister Christian," Elan adds, looking directly at me, "Miss Lottie told me to tell you she discovered the answer to her question. You know . . . about what to do . . . about things. She said this book holds the key to solving a sort of dilemma you two shared."

"Thank you, Elan. I think I understand."

"Only one way to know for sure what she meant."

"What's that?"

"Read the book."

With personal delivery of the manuscript complete, and arrangements made for the next morning, Vikki, Elan and Mercher depart for the evening. I exit the pub through the large double doorway leading to the hotel lobby to check in.

Moments later, upon entering my room, I see my bags stacked neatly in a comfortable-looking chair just inside the door. A small, round wooden table is next to the chair. It has a petite porcelain reading lamp on it. Hanging above the chair is a small old-fashioned looking clock. An oak coat rack with dull brass hooks stands in the corner. I gently lay the binder and manuscript next to the lamp and hang up my coat and hat as I survey the rest of my accommodations. On the adjoining wall is the entrance to a small bathroom. Past the bathroom, along the same wall, is a single bed and a nightstand that matches the table by the door. On the nightstand is a telephone, a glass pitcher filled with water and a tall glass with an etched floral pattern along the base, matching that of the pitcher.

The space is warm and inviting and will be more than adequate for my purposes. French doors, on the far wall beyond the bed, lead to an ornate balcony I saw from the street. I cross the room and peer outside. In nicer weather, this would be an inviting perch from which to view the promenade. Today, however, the storm brings shears of rain relentlessly bombarding this side of the building. I stare out for a few minutes at passersby, braving the harsh conditions for whatever reasons. I am glad to be in my room, finally alone.

Parched, and exhausted, from the combination of an ample amount of alcohol and intense conversation, I pour a glass of water from the pitcher and make my way over to the chair. Finishing half the water at once, I place the glass on the table, toss my luggage to the floor and lower my tired frame into the inviting cushion. I am exhausted; not only from the day, but also from the circumstances of the journey. The moment overwhelms me, my head feels light. *I should have had more to eat and less to drink.* Everything is so surreal, yet I know it is very real and these people are real and this place was real for Lottie when she was here. Tomorrow I hope to meet others who worked with her, anyone who knew her and how she was during her last days here. Tonight though, I seek only to understand the message she wanted me to know. Could this ancient writing be the key to the mystery I have been trying to unravel in my mind? Could it have the answers to all the questions tormenting me, disrupting my sleep? Turning on the lamp and reaching for the manuscript Elan's words echo in my head. '*Read the book.*'

Fear agus déithe
(Men and gods)

Translated from the ballads

Proem

Brothers and sisters,

Heed the ink which stains this parchment, for it tells a sad, dark truth. Revealed through ballads sung near a warm fire, is this lesson from mother to daughter: The world is ever changing before us, around us and after us, just as the spring waters erupt from its source, cutting through rock and sand, causing the earth to concede. As time passes, we observe the river whole, flowing on to the great sea into vastness. But from where does the spring water come? To where does the sea flow? Those who seek to understand, will. Those who do not, will not matter.

This thought comes to me as revelation after many years on this earth: We are all travelers, mere visitors of this world, bound together by spirit. Our lives are just a small portion of a larger creation, which is more than we are, with no beginning or end. Our time in this world is but an instant, and how we choose to spend it defines us in the end. All the world is comprised of diverse political and religious ideologies, and people of various cultures from all corners of the earth which, when brought together, define our uniqueness as humans. Herein now, I say to you in truth, no single color defines the rainbow. The Creator's covenant is whole only when each part is included. Therefore, I say, as we live, we must learn to embrace the unknown to us, the new, to accept our fears of such as lack of understanding, and face our story, tread our path, with an open mind. For where understanding and acceptance is lost, so dies the soul of man.

Faithfully,

John Douglas

Vicar of St. German

The 17th day of March 1245 Anno Domini

Land of Illusion

Betwixt the heavens and hell
Exists the darkest delusion
A place where undead anguish eternal
Bode ill in the land of illusion

Brilliant, intermittent flashes of light illuminated blackened skies while earth-shaking explosions of thunder rumbled continuously amidst torrential rain. Howling gusts of wind cried in eerie chorus, as if God's full fury and rage was damning every living thing in its path. The sea heaved with dark waves rising and crashing onto jagged rocks and boulders lining the shore. From a distance, a young Gorry could see ghostly hollow-faced figures floating along the edge of the nearby cliff; lost spirits with no eyes or noses, whose mouths were nothing but dark ovals. They were without clothing, their bodies lacking any identity, instead appearing covered only by bluish-gray rotting skin dripping from their bones. As he continued to watch this hellish scene unfold he knew he had been here before. Between each gust, he could hear their haunting cries like an eerie discord in an unrecognizable distorted pitch, intensifying with each flash of light as the clouds relentlessly dispensed every drop of water the heavens could hold. As the gruesome drama played on, he became aware of two misshapen silhouettes near those lamenting spirits. They appeared to him to be in some great conflict with each other. Young

Gorry rubbed his sleepy eyes, trying to focus on the commotion still some distance away. When the next flash of light burst it illuminated the two shadowy figures, revealing their identities. Gorry could see the face of his father distorted with torment. A few feet from his father, he could see his mother, Iniuria, her expression one of fear as she cowered on the ground with arms and hands raised to shield herself.

"Fides!" Gorry cried out to his father. "Fides, why?"

The flash quickly departed, engulfed by darkness as a loud booming clap shook the earth. Voices of spirits continued their lamentation as Gorry's body rose from the ground, weightless, floating like an apparition. A distinct crisp sound, like nothing he had heard before, made a whining wisp then a snap. With the next flash Gorry found himself returned to the ground, much closer to his father. The spirits wailed and moaned louder and their heads turned from side to side conferring with each other in anguished accord, horrified by what they witnessed. He could see his father's eyes changing rapidly before him, fading into the same dark pools as the eyes of the spirits. Only a small, brilliant beam of light, no larger than the head of a pin, shone from the center of each oval. He could hear his father snarling as if a wild dog now possessed him. He watched as his father's flesh receded, revealing only bones covered by a thin bluish-gray veil. Another round of deafening thunder rolled across the sky. Another flash, close and so brilliant, offered a new look on his father's face. It had become as hollow as the spirits surrounding him.

"Father . . . Mother!" Gorry cried out again. "What is happening? Why are the heavens so angry? Why are we here? What have we done to make the spirits weep over us so?" Then he shouted into the celestial abyss beyond the cliff. "Mannan, if you are always present, be here with me now, save me from this hell. Why have you let this happen? What sins have been committed? What evil is this? I don't understand."

He fell to his knees and prayed. "Great Spirit. If you are there, bring me peace. Wake me from this vision."

"You . . . !" his father roared, looking upon his son still speaking in a voice unlike his own. "You are not my son. You believe a world you cannot see will protect you. While the fate of your birthright slowly dies, you are none the wiser. Blindness enshrouds and entombs you. It makes you a fool!"

His father raised his arm ready to strike and Gorry fell to the ground. Another intense flash sliced through the darkness. The earth below his feet trembled once more. His father moved closer to the cliff, peered over, then backed away quickly. The storm raged on as the spirits wailed even louder than before.

Through the constant flashes of illumination Gorry saw his ghostly father pushing his mother to the ground.

"Please, no more. I beseech you!" she begged. "Our world evolves as we live. Accept it! Embrace the changes. Reap the harvest! We have no obligation to the laws of old. They no longer apply. Your beliefs are dying and your world with it!"

"And you!" his father condemned, "You have broken

the covenant, betrayed your family and fallen prey to the weakness of your desires. You carry the seed of your disgrace within you, dooming yourself to an unthinkable position. You have squandered our station, ruining our family name forever."

He pointed to Gorry as he spoke to Iniuria. "You are no longer our son's mother. You have chosen to follow the lawless, making them your masters, letting them destroy our land and our ways. If you, whom I have always felt were above all others, are nothing other than a slave of man and their new ways . . . then you are no longer my wife."

His father raised a long, narrow stick made of alder wood, carved with letters and symbols, and shook it. "Woman, gaze upon this stick."

"No!" she screamed, covering her eyes with her forearm. "Please, no!"

"Gaze upon this stick, woman," he commanded again. "Gaze upon it so you may be measured."

For a moment, all light vanished. Gorry heard a chilling anguished shriek cut through the void, trailing off into the darkness. With the next lighted glimpse, Gorry could see only the shadowy figure of his father, looking over the edge of the cliff. The spirits appeared frantic amidst the chaos, pointing into the stormy sky as well as to the raging sea below. Their faces now full of horror and sorrow as they watched his father in disbelief. Gorry felt himself rising again, much higher than before. From this elevation, he could see his mother slumped upon the ground, her gown drenched with rain. She had not gone over the cliff as he thought.

The storm suddenly ceased, void of all sounds and light save a single constant beam piercing through blackness, revealing only what Gorry looked upon. He felt nothing as his body stayed there, hovering. Neither his father, mother, nor the spirits, could see him from his new vantage point. Gorry's father stood between his mother and the spirits floating past the edge of the cliff; the spirits seemed to be beckoning him to follow. As swiftly as Gorry had ascended, he descended and was once more on the ground, closer to his mother's side. He looked into her face, into her sullen eyes. She wept inconsolably and said nothing. Her long, yellow hair draped around her shoulder, partially covering her swollen belly. He wanted to reach out to her but could not.

"My son," she sobbed staring at the ground.

He felt her suffering, her pain, and his heart broke for her. "You will always be my mother," Gorry cried.

There was no reply as she kept her head bowed in shame. The storm returned with full fury now as Gorry rose from his mother's side and charged toward his father, heart pounding, fists clenched ready to strike. As he approached, ready to push his father from the cliff's edge, another flash illuminated the sky revealing his father's face again, this time distorted with great sorrow and defeat, not hate and vengeance as it once was. Gorry's chest heaved with every breath. Confusion consumed him. His eyes now desperately scanned the landscape for his mother again. Where had she gone?

Gorry stood helpless as his father turned his back to

the sea and raised his arms skyward. Looking past Gorry he shouted.

"Will no one watch with me this hour? Is my life only to be imagined?"

Gorry yelled to him. "I am here with you, Father!"

His father continued to speak as if he had not heard him. "I have been betrayed. My vanity has distorted my reason. Care not of my passing. Great God Odin, I beseech you, come hither and guide me to Valhalla."

"Father, I am here with you!"

"Mona . . . my beautiful lily of the pond," his father said sorrowfully, still gazing beyond. Finally, looking directly into Gorry's eyes, his father uttered, "Forgive me my son."

Gorry lurched forward, reaching out to him as his body fell backward off the cliff, his image swallowed by the dark abyss.

Vivid, distressing images lingered in Gorry's mind as he abruptly awoke, chest still heaving as it had while he dreamt. Clods of soil and crumpled leaves fell from his hair and clothes as he sat up straight in his bed on the soft moss groundcover. He had experienced this otherworld, this land of illusion, many times since childhood: a world where he could interact with undead souls caught between life and death. He wondered for a moment of what was real and what was imagined. Listening to the early morning theater of chirping birds, the rustling of small creatures, and the sound of morning dew trickling from branch to branch until finally tumbling to the earth below, assured him he had returned to the reality of the living; he was home in his glen.

It was natural for Gorry to sleep in a certain position, so when he awoke he would face the sea, in order to be inspired at first sight of the vast eternity surrounding this tiny island that was his domain. His home at the base of this majestic glen, with all of its grace and beauty, was his place to be one with God's creation. Gorry loved to inhale the sweet aroma of damp foliage that filled this serene place. He loved listening to the rushing waters in the nearby stream, flowing from the mountains through the glen as they cascaded over rocks that bordered the banks and served as small impediments to the charging current, creating placid pools of water to nourish the wandering and the thirsty. The glen was Gorry's world. Producing all things of itself, it was his Avalon. Here he was content.

When Gorry determined the moment was well, understanding his abrupt wakening was due solely to his imagination, he rose to prepare for his journey. Gathering the few pelts he would need for bartering, he thought about the path he would travel today. It would take him from this haven, leading him north through the misty glen. It would wind through a dark forest filled with a silent army of cedars, spruces, fir, oak, sycamore, and beech. These were soldiers, he imagined, casting their ominous shadows year-round, creating a habitat for all. The path would pass through open fields and peaceful farmlands. It would ascend nearby hills, until finally descending into the pinnacle of civilization: a settlement at the edge of St. Patrick's Island named Holmtown. Gorry did not travel to the settlement often, as he did not care for the things of man and the callous and way they were encroaching on nature.

As he started out, Gorry knew he must be cautious traveling the earthen route fraught with ruts and slopes; many shared the footpath weaving through this land, both friend and foe. It was a course flanked with an endless inventory of potential predators, who preyed upon the innocent for nourishment. It rendered man vulnerable, precariously surviving only by his understanding of his place within the hierarchy.

As Gorry made his way along the side of the glen to find a narrower crossing up stream, he passed a place where flowing water had spent much time cutting through black rock. From where he stood, he could see water gushing from a fall into a gentle, dark pool. Giant moss-covered boulders surrounded the pool as if protecting it from harm. An abundance of smaller, dull-gray rocks lay in clumps of floral-like protuberances all around, accented by cousin stones that were also gray and sparkled with luster. Above the falls, he could see several fallen trees lying among the ferns, creating a natural bridge that would allow him safe crossing, provided they were sturdy enough and not rotted by time and moisture. It was here by the falls he knew to watch out for the Spirit of Man. Real or imagined, the Spirit was known by his shaggy hair and bushy beard. He measured only half the height of a regular man and was revered by all, for he alone possessed the power to reverse enchantments cast by other creatures. The Spirit had no patience for folly so only those in the most dire situations dared to seek him out. It was the Spirit's choice to either show compassion and remove any curse cast on a person or uphold the revenge of whomever had unleashed it: more often, he chose the latter. Gorry had seen the Spirit here before, but not today.

The Fortunate Isle

A gift to please all earthly needs
Bestowed upon this garden grand
'Tis Mona whole in all things required
Bless those who suckle her splendid land

Once past the falls, the darkness of the shaded glen gave way to a more open forest with a gentle stream winding through it. Winter had finally begun to show signs of retreat as milder temperatures ushered in the promise of life anew. An array of multicolored buds burst from every tree, lush green plants sprang from beneath their blanket of leaves, and flowering vegetation was giving birth all around.

Standing alone at the edge of the woods, Gorry felt the comforting presence of the earth, sea, sun, moon, and wind, reminding him at once he was but a small being living at the feet of divine spirits within this marvelous creation.

"Great Spirit," he whispered to the sky. "Come hither and be with me this day. Be my guide as I travel the road of deception and face the enemies of our land."

As Gorry followed the path through the forest, mist filled the air, moistening his clothing. Soon a dense fog floated between the trees. Flowing waters of the stream played a familiar tune; a delightful jig. Beyond a grove of shrubs Gorry noticed what appeared to be a void between the stream and nearby rocks. A space lacking color where objects were not so clearly defined except by imagination: where one senses, rather than sees. It was here Gorry became aware of a small clan of fair people: spirits, secondary divinities. Their tiny unclothed bodies gently danced about as they spoke to each other in hushed soft voices, interrupted infrequently with hardy rounds of laughter. Gorry knew of these people, however, he had only seen them on certain rare occasions such as today, when the morning haze flooded the land, causing the stark colors of contrast to disappear. He hid behind a tree, so as not to disturb them.

Watching them cavorting about in their seemingly innocent pomp, Gorry wandered off into a daydream in which he envisioned the full glory of the earth, sea, and sky. He wondered if he was in heaven itself. "The An Domhain." He uttered in amazement. Even though spoken only as a whisper, his voice drifted through the silent air and was heard by the keen old man of the fair people, whose name was Prettanike. Prettanike was a fierce warrior and ruler since the beginning of time itself, who lived out his years doting over his family of five daughters. He was greatly respected by all. Those who spoke of him feared him as a god. Sensing Gorry's presence, Prettanike stirred from his throne of rocks in the pool of water, moaning several times to alert the tiny spirits, warning any impending marauders of his presence. When all was silent again, Prettanike returned to his seat to admire his progeny. Gorry peeked out from behind the tree to gaze upon the sisters. Of all five the two sisters, Hibernia and Britannia, were of direct descent. The three others, who were adopted by Prettanike, were Andium, Sark and Mona. Sark's twin Alderney was taken in infancy: it is said her soul still lives within Sark. The world both adored and coveted the beauty and grace of the sisters; making them vulnerable in many ways, even while always under the watchful eyes of Prettanike. Of all the sisters, Gorry favored Mona, desiring her the most. He studied her closely, observing her place among the others, feeling the beating of his heart increase until he could watch no more. As he looked away into the depths of the forest, he was overwhelmed and disturbed by his vision of her.

He thought about her in this place. *If I could come this close to you, to see you in this most defenseless way, could someone else, a demon soul perhaps, get as close? My fear for you grows. How well are you truly guarded by Prettanike? How defenseless are you?*

As the air began to warm, the mist, so worshipped by Gorry, dissipated. Streaks of sun illuminated the woods here and there restoring the contrast of defining lines and shadows. He observed the limbs of trees and shrubs being warmed on one side by emerging sunlight, while those on the other side of the same remained shaded. With color returning to the forest, Gorry's vision of the fair people faded away. His daydream dispensed, renewing a sense of clarity between what was imagined and what was real.

"Great Spirit!" he cried again, to the sky. "You have taken my shield, the mist. I have become defenseless to the alluring beauty of this isle, exposed to all her natural splendor."

With the vision of the fair people only a memory,

Gorry continued on his way. He was aware he must keep his eyes on the path in front of him to maintain balance. He must look along the pathway to prepare for the possibility of coming upon obstacles such as those fallen by nature or misfortune, or those creatures whose timing to wander the same route was a coincidence that may result in unwanted confrontation.

The shield of the forest now gave way to long, wide valleys winding through majestic mountains to the east, each crest increasingly higher until reaching the summit in the center of the isle, and with open fields rolling across nearby hills to the west. To the north were fertile fields. Nature providing of its own accord, grains, grapes, apples, wood, and herbs. This truly was the fortunate isle, happy and blessed. Gorry traveled north along the western ridge, away from the mountains toward a small line of hills lining the sea. He could hear the perpetual striking of waves on the rocks below, as he followed the path along one section of this ridge where a cliff dropped sharply to the shore. Gorry stopped among a line of flowery ledges and jutting stones where the herring gulls nested. He looked down at the endless line of narrow beaches and precipices following one another into what seemed infinity. On a clear day, from the cliffs' edge, he could gaze across the sea upon the mass of a majestic granite mountain range of another land, although today it was still shrouded in early morning mist.

Beyond the first ridge, parallel to the sea, the hills receded into a lush green valley spattered with proud gorse and lavish heather. Gorry traveled along the side of this hill and into the valley. The path, used mainly by animals to navigate around groves of thick shrubs, thorns, and vines, was barely conspicuous in the matted grass bed upon which it lay. Gorry had not been through this valley for some time but knew this path would take him to his destination quickly.

Traversing the narrow lane, he thought about the nature of his expedition. Today he was on his way to a wake and a funeral. Word had reached him, as it normally did by way of travelers who passed through the head of the glen on the trail from Castletown, of the death of a man Gorry had learned much about. He had been told the man who died came into the world fatherless. His mother had taken him away from Holmtown as soon as he was born, going north to the village of Ramsey where she had family. There, she raised him until he turned old enough to work. He was a kind and earnest young man, slightly younger than Gorry, and was very well liked in the village. By a very early age, through his wisdom, hard work and dedication, he had become a ranking member of the masons' guild. Those who knew him, or knew of him, always spoke well of him. Gorry felt the young man a kindred spirit in some way and therefore chose to leave the serenity of his home and pay his respects.

As Gorry wound his way along the trail, a flock of stonechats would occasionally burst into flight upon hearing the rustling of leaves or grass, and then dart back and forth as if to avoid attack before settling again not far from where they launched. The sweet scent of heather greeted him as he approached the valley. The gorse glowed like a welcoming warm fire for a weary traveler. His weary feet paused for a moment. Natures' own celebration of spring surrounded him. A swarm of bees busily danced around the sea of sapphire and gold in flawless synchronization. Skylarks and meadow pipits engaged in primal mating rituals. Soon, if not already, their nests would be full of the promise of new life. The shrill call of a nearby chough filled the air. Gorry watched as several ravenous black birds plucked meat from the bones of some small innocent creature. Above, a peregrine circled before rapidly swooping in for his fair share, causing the black birds to abandon their newly discovered feast and shoot into the air in unified acrobatic flight.

Gorry thought about the wonder of nature and the evolution of life. *From God comes life. From life comes death, but from death comes life again. It is true of nature and of man. We are the same.*

Continuing his journey through pastures thickly starred with budding red campion and primrose on broken ground dense with briar and hemp, he passed over small crests. The sky brightened and warmed the air arousing the sweet fragrance of honeysuckle.

As Gorry descended from one crest into an indentation filled with thick vines, he observed a stubbin clenching a limp field mouse in his jaws. The tailless cat, a rumpy, had captured the mouse as his prisoner. By some grand design, this creature was something of a cross between a female cat and buck rabbit, which had come to rule the land. Whether genuine native or from another shore was debatable. The rumpy's head was smaller in proportion to its short body. The hind legs considerably longer than those in front. The only indication of a tail was just a tussock of fur about an inch in length, like that of a rabbit.

The captured mouse, whose home was and always had been here, was subject to the merciless laws of the invader. The rumpy spared no step in his evil play, carefully placing the prisoner on the ground holding his tail then beating the small prey with his other paw, slashing the flesh with nails extended.

"Daunee!" Gorry called out in a demanding voice to cease the immediate torture, causing the cat to dash away with his meal, assuredly doomed, dangling from his mouth.

"You are like other predators who come to this Island to plunder its treasures and fulfill their own desires. You capture the innocent unaware, torturing them until you are satisfied. And, when you've had your pleasure, you move on to the next and the next destroying each innocent one as you go."

Ascending the next summit, Gorry thought, *this land is pure. The plow has never been driven over these slopes. The creeks have never been quayed by permanent structures. This part of creation remains untouched by man and his domesticated beasts. The beautiful yellow cushag flourishes.*

Gorry knew the world was changing around him, around his glen. He had seen men abandon traditional methods of living as part of the wilderness, withdrawing and regathering to regions where nourishment and comfort were more easily obtained, requiring less effort. Gorry feared the ever-growing encroachment of these new inhabitants: their new lifestyles might someday reach to this hallowed ground as well. Nevertheless, for now, at least, it remained pure.

Atop this peak, to his left toward the sea, were the sacred woods south of Holmtown, home to one of the fabled bugganes. This hairy beast was said to have a crown of coarse black hair, eyes like torches, and glittering sharp tusks. Gorry remembered a story he had heard of the feared buggane who, having no liking for lazy people, tried to throw a housewife over the waterfall for putting off baking until after sunset. The woman only survived by cutting her apron strings loose to escape. Gorry believed a buggane would punish people that had offended him so he moved hastily around the sacred woods, hoping to avoid an encounter. He marched on toward a large treeless mountain, dressed only in gardens of heather, heath, and primroses, that lay between him and his destination. He thought, *how odd the behavior of the buggane*. As real as the consequences of one seemed, no man had ever actually proved their presence.

Gorry made his way along a well-defined sheep path scattering ewes and lambs as he crossed the hilltop meadow. Upon reaching the edge of the hill Gorry looked out over the landscape before him, at the small settlement of Holmtown nestled peacefully below. By this time of day, the mist protecting the Island from unwanted spirits had rolled out to sea, revealing single-storey buildings made of brick and stone with straw-thatched roofs. Muddy streets drew lines between the neatly placed structures. A large encampment had been set up just outside the village for travelers coming to attend the wake. Gorry watched the movement of carts, horses, goats, and people strolling through the main passage of the settlement. He remembered spending much of his time as a small boy living near the church, in a shelter built for orphans, and was familiar with the village and its kind, hard-working people. He looked forward to seeing some familiar faces on this visit; particularly a young woman whom he had admired from afar when they were children. She was a pretty maiden with fair hair who would come from her home on the eastern shore to spend summer months helping her uncle at the church. He hoped she might be here. Perhaps she might speak to him and he might try to speak to her without stumbling over his words. He remembered her lovely face and graceful, charming voice. He recalled, once, he had been so bold as to leave a yellow flower at her doorstep then ran away fast so as not to be seen.

Across a rivulet from the settlement, was the construction site of a new cathedral on a small rocky island, floating in the bay, connected only by a small plank pathway. At high tide, the water in the rivulet was very deep. At low tide, the channel was dry, or at least mostly. On the small floating island named for a holy saint, laborers working on the cathedral had established their own encampments. Now, with the news of the deceased, merchants from all over, as well as local villagers, set up temporary booths to sell their goods and wares to the mourners who would be attending the wake and funeral.

As Gorry looked down on the settlement and the site of the cathedral he knew he had reached his destination. The purpose of this journey, though, lay heavy on his heart. Today was a day to celebrate death. The death of a young man who had much good in his heart: one struck down too soon. *How? Why do things like this happen?* With a heavy sigh, he plodded on.

The Shrine of Saint Dachonna is Broken

Of stone and brick and mortar dry
Laid claim by sacred token
Burgled by man to call his own
The shrine of Saint Dachonna Broken

With great sorrow in his heart, Gorry crossed the plank pathway of the rivulet to the tiny island, which lay as an appendage beside the whole of Man, to the site of the unfinished cathedral. Since the beginning of time as far as any man knew, men had built holy shrines and markers in this very place. Gorry looked around, thinking. *Saint Dachonna's shrine is once again broken by the Gentiles. This is the way of men: Build. Lay waste through age and disrepair, then abandon, then demolish. Then, build again over the existing site as if it all were of no matter. How many more times will man build only to tear down for the sake of self-proclaimed triumph, and at what cost? How many more times will history be erased and replaced?*

Standing in front of the new construction, Gorry wondered why every structure built by religious organizations made to worship a trinity was erected with four sides. He walked around the new edifice slowly to gaze upon its foundation and to seek a possible meaning of the fourth. *First one must believe, then one must have faith, third one must have hope, so what holds the three together? Perhaps,* he contemplated, *only their messiah and the Great Spirit know.* Beneath the foundation Gorry saw the dungeons, places of penance below the church, which contained several dark and horrid cells. Most had nothing in them to either sit or lie on, others only a small piece of brickwork. Some were lower, darker and mustier than others; however, all chambers constructed were more than dreadful enough for any crime humanity was capable of being guilty of. It would be sheer misery for even the strongest constitution of men to sustain the murky dampness of the cavern, even for a few hours, much less for months and years, as was the punishment sometimes decreed.

Gorry had studied the ancient texts, he understood when cathedrals were erected the dungeons were built first, prior to the sanctuary itself, to remind workers of the consequence of disobedience. Gorry thought of the ancient theologian Pelagius. Pelagius did not agree with the idea of original sin. He insisted God made human beings free to choose between good and evil. He believed sin was a voluntary act. Other religious philosophers asserted that man was born into sin and would always be sinful by nature. Either way, Gorry thought, *Sin is disobedience to God, and disobedience must be punished. That is still the message being preached. Only, the definition of what is good and what is evil, what is sinful or not keeps changing, depending on who is in control. The purpose of the whole then, must be to symbolize power of the current figures of authority. Conceivably then the four sides represent the trinity: belief, faith, and hope, all held in place by the fourth wall, obedience.*

As he worked his way carefully around the transept

to the south aisle, he saw that decorative red stones were set differently from gray stones of a variety of sizes and shapes, creating a wall bordered with five lancet window sills and frames. This mixture of colors and shapes had a pleasing effect, giving a richness and variety to the building. The edifice was not large and was built in the form of a cross. With the nave and choir being longer than the transepts, appearing much the same as a body with arms outstretched.

Along the west end, around a small encampment near the sea, Gorry noticed an eclectic band of laborers and artisans, celebrating the dead man by playing a lively tune. The mourners kept rhythm on framed drums made of stretched goatskins while others played small harps, flutes, and psaltery. The music was bright and the rhythm encouraged listeners to dance or tap their toes. Gorry knew it was time to join them and pay his respects.

Three days the body had been laid out on a table within the canvas of a large tent, for there were no permanent structures outside the settlement except the cathedral still under construction. Gorry entered the cover of this canvas to give homage to the remains of the man whose time was ended too soon. Mourners entered to leave coins in a wooden bowl, which had been placed on the deceased's chest and lay food around his body; both to be used in his next life. As Gorry approached the figure lying flat and lifeless on the table before him all became silent as in his dream. The dead man's hair had been combed with lard to hold it in place. His nails were trimmed and painted to cover the black tips of his fingers.

He was smartly dressed in a white linen shirt adorned with black ribbons. A clay pipe was lying diagonally on his chest above the small wooden bowl. Candles burned all around dripping melted wax onto the floor below, puddling and cooling into solid mounds. There were those who entered the tent and began to sob. Others averted their gaze as they approached the body. All paying homage in their own way.

After a while, a man dressed in a dark robe covered from head to toe entered the tent and begin to mumble. Gorry was drawn to this mourner for reasons he did not know. He held a long narrow stick made of alder wood carved with letters and symbols.

"Sir, did you know this man?" asked Gorry.

The man did not answer.

"Sir, did you know this man?"

The man only continued to mumble, so Gorry asked a third time, this time his voice more commanding than questioning.

"Sir, did you know this man!"

At that he stopped his mumbling. Then in a feeble, quiet voice said, "This man was conceived in sin by lustful desire, but died in humble service to his maker. Now, he joins me in the House Beneath the Hill. The path to the otherworld has been cleared." He laid the stick beside the body, then carefully brought it back to his side. "He has been measured. Now he is prepared to return to the earth from whence he came. His decaying body will soon release seeds of light."

Gorry recognized these words and understood the

man was giving the deceased instructions on how to get to the next world.

"But, did you know his name?"

"There are no names, save one, which we came from and then return again."

An old woman standing nearby, who had heard the interaction, spoke. "The name you seek is given us at birth to assign our place in this world. He needs a name no more. For he will join us and The Dark Man, to comfort and sing to the souls of the dead in the Summerlands of the Otherworld."

A loud noise outside the tent shattered the reverence of the moment. Curious, Gorry went out to see what it was. As it happened, a pig had gotten loose from its pen and ran into a booth filled with cooking pots and utensils causing quite a commotion. When he reentered the death tent, the man and woman were gone.

Gorry looked around. To his left, on a table, there was an assortment of clay pipes and tobacco, the use of which was said to keep evil spirits from finding the deceased. At the far end of the table was a single mercury clock that had been manually disabled; stopped at the time of death. This gesture made to indicate, at least for the deceased, the hands of time stood still.

He thought, *Life, so precious, was simplified by this basic manipulation. Is this all life meant? Time reduced by fractions, swiftly, deliberately, ticking away until it inevitably ceases.*

He chose a pipe, filling and pressing fragrant tobacco into the bowl. Once lit, the pleasant aroma wafted through the air encircling the space around him.

An old woman wearing a dark scarf over her head sat quietly in a corner near the entrance. After a moment, she began to recite a poem.

> *A son is born, a life begins.*
> *Then life is taken. So, it ends.*
> *Struck too soon before his time.*
> *Leaving those he loved behind.*
> *All around the living weep.*
> *The flock has lost another sheep.*
> *His mother in her anguish moans.*
> *A part of her will now lay with stones.*
> *Her love for him still lingers on.*
> *For he will always be his mother's son.*

At the end of the poem, the woman sobbed softly as she swayed back and forth, tightly clutching her scarf. Beside the old woman stood a small boy, dressed in torn, stained rags made from sackcloth, whose dirt-smudged face resembled the face of the dead man and whose eyes were moist with sorrow. As Gorry stood there watching the two of them, he was struck by a strange thought. The once warm pipe filled with tobacco and fire, sending swirls of smoke and fragrance into the air had gone out and was now nothing more than an empty vessel. Not unlike the cold body lying before him, which had once been full of life and had a fire burning within. Now it lay silent, empty.

As Gorry walked toward the opening of the tent to

return the pipe for the next mourner's use and leave, the old woman reached out her arm and spoke.

"Leece," she said.

He stopped, looked at the woman's face and into her sullen weeping eyes. His heart lurched within him in a hauntingly familiar way. What was it in her voice, her face, her eyes? She spoke again, looking at the deceased.

"My son. His name was Leece. He was my youngest son. I once had another, but he was taken from me when still a child. This boy is my grandson; he was born blind. God has punished him for my sins. His father, Leece was born cursed because of my immoralities and so now, this child suffers."

Consumed with compassion for them, yet knowing he had few words to ease their grieving, Gorry gently patted the child on the head. "Do not worry, God will protect you," he said. Placing the pipe on the table, he walked out of the tent and into the smothering sounds and smells of the festival of death.

Music and conversation, interrupted by random cheers coming from spectators watching an array of entertainers, filled the air as crowds mindlessly weaved their way from one booth to another in search of some trinket or treasure. This event, to mark the passing of a soul from this world to the next, was not the solemn occasion Gorry had imagined it would be, rather one of dizzying merriment; unsettling his mind and soul.

A short distance from where Gorry was observing these happenings, beside one of the tents, stood a slender young woman with a fair face. Her eyes were the color of the sea on a clear summer's day. Her straight golden hair was tied loosely on top of her head. A few strands had escaped and hung freely, dancing around her rosy cheeks, while others dangled upon the curve of her neck. Her name was Aine Douglas. Her family lived along the eastern shore of the main island where they owned farmland in the north, near the village of Ramsey. They were successful merchants, owning a large trading and import company. She and her brothers had traveled from their home shore to this small island rock to visit their uncle and see the new cathedral being constructed.

Aine noticed Gorry immediately, thinking him a handsome curiosity; his black locks of hair falling loosely around his shoulders. She thought his piercing dark green eyes were utterly captivating; nevertheless, she could not quite determine what it was she saw in them. Was it deep compassion or worldly innocence? Perhaps both? His nose was straight and in good proportion, complementing his face very nicely and accentuating strong lips beneath. She admired the rugged curve of his chin defined with a deep-set dimple. His broad shoulders and muscular upper arms were the perfect resting place, she decided, for such a handsome head. Her interest of this young man she had known since childhood was overwhelming, so she decided to make her way through throngs of people and introduce herself. Maybe, she imagined, she could accompany him; assist in navigating his way around the village and cathedral grounds. As Aine maneuvered through the sea of festival merriment, her heart began to beat ever faster. However, when she eventually made her way to where Gorry had been standing, he was no longer there. Her eyes darted back and forth trying to catch a glimpse of him. Where might he have gone? For several moments, Aine searched the crowd to no avail.

Gorry, unaware of Aine's presence and intentions, passed through the festival tents and booths to what seemed to be a central location. Here many villagers had gathered to sell fruits, vegetables, and herbs grown and harvested from small family gardens, as well as fish caught only hours earlier. His mouth watered as he breathed in the scent of freshly roasted meats and boiling stews. With his next breath, the aroma of warm bread and fruit pies filled his senses. Trading one of his pelts for a loaf of bread and a bit of roasted rabbit from one of the stands, he satisfied his hunger.

Beyond the market, Gorry could see where the sarcasms were acted out under the protection of an outer ring of merrymakers. Curious, Gorry made his way to the large barn. Inside, throughout the structure, hung branches of evergreen: festoons of laurel and holly. At the center of the theater Gorry witnessed a great assemblage of human disdain. In the middle was a man clothed in a brightly-colored red tunic layered over a long, white linen shirt. His head was adorned with a dark blue turret hat; his feet with black ankle boots. A large belt around his waist displayed a blue and green peacock feather. He stood under an awning of hay held high over his head, like palm fronds, by four sentries dressed only in braies. He announced he was the teacher of the game. All at once, he ordered all the men out of the center of the acting area.

The men gleefully ran from the theater to a corner of the barn, discussing which one would play the part of the bull. The teacher then called to some young girls in another corner of the barn to enter the acting area, which he called the pasture. A young girl pranced to the focus point of the room draped only in an animal hide, which barely covered her back and shoulders, and nothing more. Horns were tied on top of her head, to simulate the appearance of a cow. Her maidens, dressed in loosely fitted, sheer, linen robes of assorted colors, came in friskily dancing around her, as a handful of musicians played a lively tune.

A loud knock was heard, created by a man pounding on a post with a large stick. The festivity gaiety stopped.

"Who dares to enter?" the teacher shouted.

"The guards demand admittance for the bull, for he is without his cow and desires milk," the men answered in unison.

Admittance was refused at first while the maidens and the cow continued to dance. The knocking repeated. Finally, the fronds were drawn erect by the sentries to signify the door had been opened and the bull could enter. The bull was also robed only with a hide and horns and was surrounded by a band of young men as his guards. They wore masks and fanciful garments. Each carried a long stick and had tied a disc of plaited straw onto his arm to represent a shield. The bull endeavored to grab hold of the cow numerous times, but each time she was defended by her maidens. During each effort by the bull, the teacher marched through the middle of the theater drinking wine from a large cup. His sentries followed carrying the fronds high above his head. After several attempts, the teacher cried out.

"Seize the present! For if not now, then when?"

A mock fight began between the guards and the maidens, who gently wrestled each other to the ground, pretending to die and fall away from the center of the theater where, finally, the bull captured the cow. The crowd cheered as they watched the bull take the cow. When the play ended, the audience dispersed forming small clusters and began engaging in intimate conversation.

As two of the players, dressed as guards, passed in front of Gorry, one of them confronted him.

"Who are you, stranger, walking among us so boldly?"

Gorry showed no fear. "I am Gorry, son of Ragnvald, Godred the Black, who was son of Olave the Red."

"A Crovan?" the man pursued.

"One of the many cousins of the royal throne?" the other man asked.

"Where are your guards then, your servants?" the first man said mockingly.

"I need no guards, nor any men to serve me," replied Gorry. "The Great Spirit Manannan is my father. I am faithful to Mona. My spirit is my shield. My wit, my defense."

The two men sneered. The one who spoke first continued.

"Well, young Manannan, son of Learr, we will agree to be your guards this day for we are already dressed as such. And in this new world, you can be anything or anyone you desire as long as you dress the part."

Two of the young girls dressed as maidens from the play came upon the men and Gorry. They were giggling and talking to each other.

"Whom do you guard?" one of the maidens asked.

Smiling, the guards played along with the jest.

"Stand back, fair maiden, for we guard a prince."

"Does the prince have a lady?" the other girl asked, looking into Gorry's eyes. "A princess perhaps? Or, would you prefer both a princess and her maiden at the same time?"

Gorry quickly grew uneasy. "I am already betrothed," he said to the surprise of the small group, which had gathered around him. "And I am loyal to none other," he said as he turned away, confident he would be left alone.

A few men from the encampment pushed their way through the crowd of onlookers that had encircled Gorry, the guards and maidens.

"Enough," commanded one of the men. "Go find another to sacrifice and return to your coven. We are this man's true guardians."

As the crowd dispersed, they jeered and taunted Gorry and his rescuers.

"Your curiosity will surely be your demise brother." One of the men continued. "These witches disguise themselves with beauty, but only gather here to feed off man's lust and greed. They do not understand loyalty to this land. Affiance such as yours is rare indeed. Come with us to the encampment near the village. Join us in celebration with the dance of Flidais, goddess of cattle and fertility. You can play the part of Ailill Finn, High King of Ireland. We shall all break bread together this night."

Gorry agreed to leave the festival and accompany them to their camp along the edge of the village where travelers and villagers alike were welcome. He followed his liberators away from the crowds and the noise back across the rivulet joining the small island to the larger.

The fringe encampment, outside the settlement, contained several small campsites full of people from all parts of the Island and other lands. A piper greeted each of the guests as they arrived. The leader of the campsite Gorry joined said a few words as each guest arrived, welcoming everyone to the supper. Once all were seated around a makeshift wooden table, he orated a thankful phrase imparting a blessing meant to sanctify the meal.

The party dined on fresh pudding made of sheep's heart, liver, and lungs, covered with onion. Gorry peeled back the stomach casing to enjoy familiar odors and tasted the nutty texture and delicious savory flavor. The table was spread with dishes of ground offal, bread, herbs, and onion wrapped in caul fat, and fried pudding made of congealed blood with oatmeal formed into sausage-like links with intestine as a casing. There were neeps and tatties enough for all. While most of the men drank wine, Gorry drank only water.

"Today we feast," said one of the men.

"And tomorrow, Father Druce plants our brother," said another.

"Do you know Father Druce?" the first man asked Gorry.

"Who doesn't know the good farmer turned preacher?" a man across the table said as he laughed.

Gorry did not answer. He knew the priest very well. After his father had perished and his mother disappeared, a young Gorry stumbled into the streets of the village to find food. Father Druce took him in to the church to give him shelter and an education. Gorry learned to read and write. His thirst for learning caused him to sneak away from his bed at night and sit in the church room of archives, reading ancient manuscripts and monks' notes. The more knowledge he gained, the more sorrow he felt: sorrow for those who could not make sense of the order of things in a world so uniquely designed and created. Father Druce was very strict. His desire to enforce obedience hastened Gorry's desire to abandon this environment for another. When Father Druce would declare his authority, which had become often, Gorry could only hear his own father's angry voice screaming into his ears. Gorry would rebuke his preaching, arguing there was only one called father, a father of all, not defined by blood or flesh; but, through faith.

From their table, Gorry and the men could hear laughter, as well as crying, waft through the air as mourners around fires on this side of the rivulet shared stories involving the deceased in a more traditional manner. Along with heartfelt poetic lamentations and boisterous songs, there were also debates. Given the current situation, of chief debate was the afterlife. Seated now around the campfire, bellies full, some asserted that a man could come back in human form or could be reawakened as an animal or plant, depending on his actions during his past life. Others argued the existence of heaven.

There was another group a short distance away, where a man who, when he stood, towered above all the other men. Black curly hair covered his head and a black beard his chin. His naturally dark skin was weather-worn from wind and sun. He wore layers of tunics, loose-fitting chausses and sandals strapped all the way from his feet to his knees. His arms were as big as a man's leg and his hands and fingers could reach around the entire skull without stretching. The local men called him the Risi, for he was a giant. Beside him was a man who stood no taller than the Risi's waist, with a large, square head noticeably disproportionate to his short body. A smooth silver beard flowed from his chin to midway down his chest. He smoked a long-stemmed pipe which never moved from his lips; even when he spoke. His name was Corkan. A third man, of average height and weight, sat by the fire near to the other two. Scars on his cheekbones and forearms told a story of torture throughout his life. The villagers said he had been born both male and female, but had been cut at birth to make him neither. He was dressed in brown linen pants and wore a tattered white shirt. They called him Saoi, for he was very wise and could see visions. He spoke in a quiet voice to the other two while poking a stick into the fire to stoke the flames. Gorry stood silently at the edge of the light from the burning fire behind him, staring through the darkness to the nearby campsite where he saw the three very distinguishable silhouettes. To him, they represented power, divinity, and knowledge.

After all the conversations and moral debates lost their intensity, the men began the ritual of acceptance, compromise and talk of future plans. One man, a man named Fin, called to Gorry, bringing him back to the campfire.

"Tomorrow will you side with us during the games?" he asked.

When Gorry saw the man, he remembered his childhood living at the church orphanage in the village. He remembered a boisterous young man named Fin, from one of the wealthiest families. Because of his family status, Fin had been afforded the best education and the opportunity to be trained in military leadership at a young age. He became a champion rider and archer. His refinement and competitive nature poured into his social status. Admired by all the young ladies, Fin could have any he wanted, and so, had several. Fin excelled in the science of politics and persuasion. Many men followed him, or would follow him, into battle. Gorry remembered thinking, even as a little boy, how different they were. He excelled in reading, writing, and studying nature and history: with no care of what others thought of him. So, when Fin asked, *'Tomorrow will you side with us during the games?'* Gorry sensed an uneasiness rather than comradery.

"Why would I fight for your victory?" he asked without thinking how it might be taken.

Another man, an acquaintance of Fin named Cowper,

from the village of Rushen, spoke. "Don't be disturbed, my friend. This man speaks of a mock battle in which we divide our clans and challenge each other only in might, without weapons."

"And what is the cause?" Gorry inquired.

"The cause is simply to remind us we are men," said Fin.

"We fight to prove we are still alive, and to win!" added Cowper. "You see, a couple of Chief Guildsmen, Greacy and Davison, have called for a judgement to be made to their issue. The law allows the issue to be resolved with the assistance of kindred, which some of us claim to be. We've traveled from the villages of Rushen and Douglas to provide support tomorrow, if called to help defend our cousins. We're civilized men for the most. Just a few good blows are all that will come of it. We also honor the deceased man by defending his good name along with our own. It's our tradition."

"And who was he to you?" Gorry asked as he looked around the fire. "Who here knew him, what he did, or where he came from?"

The men looked around at each other confused. They thought Gorry knew his identity. Their voices grumbled with questions of their misconception.

Then Gorry explained to the men. "I only know of him: of his hardships. I heard how he overcame the shame others made him feel all his life, simply because he was born without a father and how he became a respected, kind man despite it. I know he dedicated his life to the construction of the new cathedral because of his loyalty to God. I never knew him; never shook his hand. I simply came to pay my respects because I believe him to have been a good man. I do not understand the levity you display at his death. I see this battle you describe as mockery portrayed to remedy to your human fears."

All the men grew silent, staring intensely at Gorry. Immediately sensing their uneasiness, and not wishing to offend his companions further or insult their traditions, Gorry quickly continued, providing them with a more noble reason to cause each other harm while honoring a man they barely knew.

"It has been said: When a warrior goes into battle, he sheds his blood for those whom he has loyalty, and those who fight with him become his blood brothers. I suggest, since this man dedicated himself to constructing a cathedral for a belief to which he was loyal, he died a warrior of God. I think that an honorable death, worthy of remembrance. Your gesture to celebrate this man then, is also noble. All who fight to honor him tomorrow will become his blood brothers."

The men raised their cups and cheered.

"But, as for me, I will not choose sides in this celebration," Gorry added.

"Not even if he was a brother?" Fin asked. "Your brother?"

Gorry looked directly at Fin, then across the many faces. Understanding what Fin was implying Gorry answered. "I feel this man is my blood brother because, I too, am loyal to my beliefs. I mourn deep within my soul, that is my way to honor him. If he was my mother's son, I do not know. But, I have heard, in the lands of the East, brothers who spill blood together have a greater bond than brothers who share a mother's milk. Tomorrow you will all gain a true brother."

Quiet spread across the men like a heavy fog rolling in from the sea, for they felt he had spoken very wisely, responding well to Fin's question.

As the men from the village dispersed and the travelers settled around the fire for sleep, Gorry felt anger begin to swell within. He did not believe in their tradition. He still believed it mockery to play out this battle. He only sought to avoid confrontation on such a night as this, not to antagonize this group of men that invited him to their fire.

From his campsite, the Risi observed the conversation between Gorry and the group of men. He admired the words of Gorry, wondering about how he might learn more of him, for he thought they both shared a similar of view. *Victory*, he thought *can often be achieved through avoidance. Civility is not gained by force; but by knowledge.*

Just beyond the shadows of men keeping warm near the fires, Aine stood with Father Druce discussing preparations for the next day's ceremonies. She, too, had observed Gorry, heard his speech, and had noticed the Risi who watched in silence.

"He speaks wisely," Father Druce said to Aine.

"Indeed, he seems to be very thoughtful, Uncle."

"He is a force with which to be reckoned though. He speaks to the creatures of nature and the otherworld."

"Do you think him evil, Uncle?"

"No, not evil."

Gorry is just still naively arrogant and unwilling to accept anything other than his own view of things, Father Druce thought.

He turned with Aine and they walked away from the edge of the encampment to their own campsite several yards away. This temporary site was set up to conduct mass when the wake and funeral concluded, since the church in the village was too small for the influx of mourners that Father Druce supposed would be attending. The Church frowned upon all the activities of the sarcasms and the sale of goods sacrificed in the name of the dead, so his camp was set up on this side of the rivulet to keep the sacred separate from the unsacred. *Today*, he thought, *the pagans occupied my tiny Island on which lay a foundation of Christianity.* He accepted the terms, while he disdained the irony.   •

Bishop Symon, who had come to oversee the construction of the cathedral, greeted Father Druce and Aine as they approached the tent. The three stood outside and watched as the last glow of the sun drifted off the edge of the earth.

Looking across the rivulet at the construction site dotted with fires, listening to the various sounds and watching the various and strange rituals of the temporary inhabitants continuing their celebration of death, Father Druce leaned over to Aine. He pointed a bent finger toward the land beyond. "That is man," he said in a dour voice.

Dannsa na Fir

The fledgling must depart
To endure life if it can
So, each of us must leave our nest
To partake in the dance of man

Morning arrived, bringing with it the expected blanket of fog, rolling into the low country, leaving a wet chill in the air and heavy-dew-moistened grass all around. The song birds had begun their ritual recital while it was still dark and the various melodies could be heard repeatedly, gently stirring souls from their slumber. At Father Druce's campsite, two deacons had awakened early and were stoking the fire, roasting meat and potatoes for their leader and guests. The rich bouquet of spices drifted into the tent, made of leather walls, in which Aine and her brothers slept. Aine, roused both by the songbirds and the aroma, stretched her arms and legs out then sat up in her sleeping accommodations on the ground, thinking how she missed her soft, warm bed at home. Her brothers were already gone, or hadn't come back last night. They were older and did what they pleased, especially when away from the watchful eyes of their parents.

Gorry, too, was awake at his camp, already sitting near the fire, stirring the ashes with a stick and missing his glen. He watched the deacons in the distance as they prepared breakfast for the father and Bishop, frequently glancing at the leather-walled tent he had seen Aine go into the night before.

A man from the village named Kaughin, who had witnessed Gorry's conversation with the men the previous night, came over to bid him good morning.

"Sleep well?" he asked, taking a seat at the fire.

"Not as good as when I am in my glen"

"Do you remember me, Gorry?"

"Yes, how could I forget? You were the only friend I had as a child. Of course, I remember you, Kaughin. It is good to see you again."

"You know Gorry . . . most of us are fishermen, farmers or merchants. We are not the warriors you spoke of last night."

"Last night, I spoke through the voice of the warrior of human spirit. His weapon is his mind, not the sword. He walks the high path. He learns to fight using the strength of forgiveness. He avoids having his pride chase his enemy, whose snare is most likely already set."

"I am sorry I misunderstood your meaning my friend." He noticed Gorry looking toward the Bishop's campsite. "Whom do you watch? The deacons?"

"I do not watch the men, I wait."

"Upon what?"

"Over there, in the distance, an angel slumbers. She is pure innocence."

"Is she comely?"

"Like a flower when it buds and then blossoms. She

is, and will always be, more beautiful than any other. She is wise and strong and gracious. I have always loved her, if only from afar."

"Does she know of your interest?"

"No, she knows me only through vague childhood memories, and the voice of others."

"Are you planning to tell her how you feel?"

"I can't. We are not of the same station in life."

"But what if you two are meant to be? What if she is waiting, hoping you will reveal your feelings? How will she ever know?"

"The cushag. She will remember the yellow cushag. You remember when I left the flower on her doorstep and then we ran away. She will remember; then she will know." Gorry said wistfully.

Back at Father Druce's campsite Aine prepared for the day. Soon she emerged from her tent to join the Bishop and Father Druce for the morning meal. As the three began to talk, Father Druce noticed Aine glancing over at Gorry's campsite.

"I don't know if you remember him, but Gorry, the man who comes to us from the glen in the south, lived here as a young child," he said to her. "The Church watched over him for several years. His father had apparently fallen off a cliff near the glen during a horrible storm and his mother disappeared the same night."

"What sorrow, Uncle," said Aine.

"Yes, very sad indeed," Bishop Symon agreed.

"We educated him, teaching him to read and to understand Latin and other languages of the isles," Father Druce continued.

"Then why did you not speak to him upon his arrival?" asked Aine.

"He learned much under our teaching, he is very wise, however, he remains a conflicted soul," Father Druce said as the three of them looked over at Gorry. "This is the best distance for us."

"Conflicted?" asked the Bishop as he leaned in closer to the fire.

"Yes, he is just like his father, who perished. He believes in God wholeheartedly, yet he does not prescribe to all the teachings of the Church. Nature is his church and the spiritual world offers him guidance and companionship."

"So, he is not of sound mind?" the Bishop Symon asked.

"On the contrary, he is a soul who is most aware of who he is, where he is, as well as all the shortcomings of those around him."

"Yet you speak not to him," said Aine. "Why?"

"Because he shows no respect for civilized man and the constructs of religion," Father Druce declared. All were silent for a moment, then he continued. "You know, Gorry's father and I were friends, acquaintances really, many years ago. When we were young, his father and I shared an affection for the same woman; Iniuria was her name. We competed often for her attention. As we grew older, he and I chose different paths. I left the farm and chose to serve the Church.

"He and Iniuria married and ran away to live among the fair people in the glen. That is where Gorry was born and lived as a young child. When civilization begin to change around him, Gorry's father was unwilling to adapt. He could not accept the new ideals of society. Gorry's mother, on the other hand, embraced the idea of progress and wanted to be part of it, which caused an irreparable rift in their marriage. One night, according to young Gorry, during a horrific storm, his father and mother had a horrible argument. No one is truly sure what happened. All we know is they both disappeared. A few days later, little Gorry wandered into the village seeking food and shelter. He told us what he could remember of that night; no child should have those memories."

"What do you mean?" Aine asked.

"Well, when he first came to live with us, he would often have nightmares," Father Druce said. "I remember he was crying out one night; I shook him until he awoke and told him to steady himself. I said, at the time, I was his father and he should obey his father and . . . well, the last words he spoke to me, were a condemnation of sorts. He said I was not his father. He said he had no father, no *'Fides.'* After which, we did not speak again. He closed himself off to the world around him. Shortly thereafter he ran away: back to the glen. Sadly, I think because of what he witnessed as a child, he has no respect for man. Nature and all of its creatures take the place of authority in his world. He chose not to live among us and still condemns our ways, our authority."

♈

North of the settlement, where the shoreline rises gently forming crags of worn, ragged earth, was a great field situated atop a wall of shallow cliffs: a symbol of fortitude. Beyond it lay pristine fertile fields of lolium and fescue, where animals grazed, and beside them freshly plowed fields, where neeps and corn would soon be planted. Upon this great field, the chieftains, their tribesmen, villagers and the curious gathered late in the morning to play out a battle meant to settle an outstanding controversy between two men. As was tradition, the outcome was to be determined by the settlement's newly appointed Minister of Justice chosen by the people to act on matters representing all tribes occurring within the limits of the settlement.

"Gather round, good men of Holmtown and invited kin!" cried out the Minister. "If any complaint be made to the magistrate of wrong done or received," he said in a voice and manner making his words sound divinely inspired, "a man shall take a stone, fix his mark upon it, then deliver it to me. By doing this, he both calls his adversary to appear and summons his witnesses." He spoke with authority, keeping the index finger of his right hand raised.

"Every man here shall keep what he possesses in peace and safety, with gratitude to Tynwald, our high court, as well as the House of Keys, established by our loving conquerors many generations ago. Today, no man lives in fear of losing what he hath, lest he give it over through consequence. For the men here are not inclinable to robbery, pilfering, or licentious living. The inhabitants of our settlement are, for the most part, religiously minded. They do much reverence to their pastors, frequenting the church, and avoiding all controversies, either ecclesiastical or civil."

All the chieftains and their men cheered as the Minister spoke.

"In ancient times, the law was not written. It was rhymed, committed to memory, from one generation to another. The laws were improved, effected by nine men appointed for such purpose by a special assembly convened by our blessed Saint Patrick. Three of these were bishops, including Patrick himself, three more were kings, including a high king. The remaining three were Brehons."

The Minister spoke with such clarity and enthusiasm, the crowd moved in tighter to hear his words and share in the jubilation.

"Our great King Harald has also his circle of Brehons to decide all matters within the territory. Each chieftain here has one or more Brehons attached to his household, to decide the quarrels of his tribe."

He paused and looked across the sea of a hundred men or more as he proudly proclaimed.

"And our village, Holmtown, has its own Minister of Justice, who, today, is given authority over them all."

When he finished speaking, all the men cheered and some threw their hats and headscarves into the air. The yelling continued for a few moments until the Minister spoke again.

"My good men, we are gathered to resolve a matter of some distress, to right the wrongs of our brothers before us and to honor the deceased man, Leece, who this day will become our blood brother eternal."

The Minister motioned for two men to come close to him.

"I bring before you today Master Robert Greacy, a new inhabitant of our fine settlement, formerly a mariner by occupation, currently operating a public house to retail alcohol. And his accuser, Master John Davison, long-time resident of the community, who also operates a public house to retail alcohol and dry goods. Both are within their rights as members of the guild to compete as merchants, so long as they self-regulate with fixed price their goods and service. Of this matter, Master Davison accuses Master Greacy, whom he says owes him a debt of three barrels he loaned to help him get a start, and an additional two he provided in good faith upon the request of Master Greacy."

The Minister paused for a moment while the crowd of men jeered. When the noise decreased, the Minister continued.

"The official grievance states: Master Davison accuses Master Greacy of having an unpaid debt. He declares Master Greacy received wine and spirits from him on credit and now fears he won't be able to repay the balance because he provides free drinks to the physician, the chaplain, and certain constables. Master Greacy has been unable to repay the loan due to his current business practice and even asked for additional supply. Master Davison, in good faith, provided additional inventory to Master Greacy, which he has also not been able to obtain compensation for. Master Davison asserts Master Greacy owes him for both the cost of the alcohol and for his hardship of lost income, proclaiming he could have sold the alcohol in his establishment at reasonable value and made a profit. Therefore, Master Davison is requesting immediate and full compensation and further demands Master Greacy charge the physician, the chaplain, and constables for all drinks from this point forward."

After saying all this, the men became unusually quiet, appearing to discuss the minute details of the affair, and understand the gravity of charges.

The Minister turned to Master Greacy. "How do you plead?"

Greacy bowed. "Your eminence, if I might be allowed to explain . . . The free drinks are provided upon request solely for the benefit of the good people of Holmtown and not by random act, sir."

"How does this benefit the people of Holmtown?"

"Well, sir, as for the physician, his role is to offer assistance to the infirmed."

"Yes, but how is giving free drink to the physician going to help the sick?"

"If the drink steadies his mind then he can diagnose

more accurately, and if it steadies the hand during surgery, then the cut is clean."

Some of the men in the crowd cheered, so Greacy went on.

"And good sirs, is it not the role of the guild to help fund the Church?"

"Yes, it is," replied the Minister. "But how is giving free drink to the chaplain helping to fund the Church?"

"Well, what the chaplain doesn't pay for his drink, can be kept in the Church treasury and used for the betterment of God's house. Based on what the chaplain drinks, that would add to quite a sum."

At this the crowd roared in agreement.

"And what of the constables? What strange justification do you offer as your defense to provide the constables free drink?"

"Well your honor, if the constables are content, then the lords are content. And, if the lords are content, the whole village is content."

After a minute of contemplation, the Minister spoke to the crowd.

"My good men," he began. "I have heard the charge from the accuser, Master Davison and I have heard the negation of the defendant, Master Greacy. Master Greacy's argument is not truly a denial, rather it offered good and sound reasoning for his deeds. However, this being the last day of celebration, it would be unsatisfyingly droll if resolution was reached here by mere compromise or impasse. Ancient law provides a term for such a conflict known as Corus Bescna, a matter of contracts and obligations. The world would be evilly situated if express contracts were not binding. So, even though Master Greacy has offered a sound explanation for his actions, in order to continue pursuing the inevitable event we anxiously await, I find Master Greacy guilty of the charge."

When this was said, the men cheered loudly in anticipation of what was to come. Greacy bowed his head. His discernment and cunning overshadowed by the levity of the situation and growing impatience of the men wanting to fight.

"Master Davison, what form of punishment shall be administered?" asked the Minister.

Davison looked at the Minister and then the crowd of men.

"I choose the board."

Greacy raised his hand, "May I request assistance from my kindred when receiving the punishment?"

"What assistance does a man require when receiving the board?" asked the Minister.

"I propose Master Davison be allowed to administer the blows only after he is able to cross my line of kindred."

The Minister turned to Davison. "Do you agree to these terms, Master Davison?"

"I agree to the accused request, provided I may be assisted by my kindred as I cross the line of his."

"Both parties have come to resolve," announced the Minister. "The matter will be settled today, upon this field. The punishment carried out at the conclusion. These men have requested assistance from their kindred to create an event of defending each of them in this matter. Orderliness is absolutely a necessity while conducting this, so I will declare, within the power of my authority, all those who participate must follow these five set rules without exception. Number one: The event begins after the horn is sounded, not before. Number two: When you're knocked down, you stay down until the event concludes: do not rise again to fight. Number three: No weapons are allowed: feet and fists only. Number four: Only family members chosen and currently on the field may join the fight; others may assist the wounded but are not allowed to join in. Number five: When the horn sounds the second time, the event is concluded, and all must stop their actions. One final word. Those that remain standing at the end, when the signal horn has sounded, shall then run to the pen, over there." He pointed to a small wooden cage in the center of the field containing a sacrificial pig covered in lard. "The kindred of the first man to capture the pig shall be declared the lords of the field."

As he spoke, all the people cheered. The Minister raised his hand to hush the crowd.

"Good men, our brother, Leece, was thought of highly within our ranks. We will miss his kindness and generosity. Before he passed, Leece addressed the guild, requesting them to make a change to the rules of this game. He implored the guild saying these games we play for the sake of tradition, should end in peace. He did not know he would be the next of us to have life swiftly taken from him; however, he did realize harmony among us was far better than discord. In honor of Brother Leece, I beseech whomever the victors are today, to consider his petition in the name of unity."

Many of the men shuffled where they stood in silent contemplation and respect.

"Kindred for both sides, gather and devise your plan quickly," the Minister declared. "Then, send your men to the four corners of the field. When the horn blows, you shall defend the good names of Greacy and Davison, and honor Brother Leece." The Minister paused, gesturing with his hands. "I have one additional requirement. You must keep on your braies and chausses. There will be no Gaesatae warriors at this gathering today."

The men laughed loudly as the Minister held up a finger and waved it back and forth.

"Be neither so proud and confident in your manliness, nor trusting in the protection of nature that you unclothe yourselves this day. Now, devise your strategy, wait for the horn, and stand ready to seize the present!"

Greacy assembled his kindred, who were from Ramsey and Holmtown. He divided them into sets considering strength, quickness and cunning to comprise each of the four groups. He then assigned each to a different corner of the field. Also on his team were Corkan and Saoi. These men would not fight, but would be consulted as wise council. Greacy ordered them to stand safely along the edge. "Today, you are my brothers. Come on the field only when you see it appropriate," he told them.

Davison gathered his kindred, who were mostly from Douglas and the castle town of Rushen, home of the king.

He divided his men by size and skill as well. On this team was Fin, known for his skill in combat and the Risi chosen for his size and strength. The small teams of men left the crowd, gathering at the four corners of the field before the starting blare of battle horn was heard.

Along the outer sides of the field were crowds of supporters, including wives, children, and even the elderly. Aine joined other young women along the far side to watch the battle play out. They liked watching the young men fight, giggling shyly about which one they thought handsome, or strong.

Gorry, who had joined Corkan and Saoi to observe the events of the day, spotted Aine across the field, his gaze, his attention, was given only to her. He did not notice the other young women whispering secrets in each other's ear, spreading a message from one to the other until finally it was whispered into Aine's ear. As she looked across the field her eyes met his for only a moment. Horribly embarrassed, he quickly looked away, turning his attention to Saoi standing stiffly upright, observing the whole field. It was a large area used for grazing cattle and was full of dips and snares. To his left, Saoi saw a space where rocks consumed an entire corner. Nothing grew there. This side of the field fell sharply into the sea. Along the same cliff's edge, he could see the far distant corner of the field. The men would have to maneuver around very tall grasses laced with vine. This area covered the top of a small rise and there was no clear path to travel. Far to the right, Saoi looked over a small dip in the field, which held water whenever it rained. Around it was thick mud and tall, thin brown grasses. Beyond the muddy shallow pond was a grove of thin white trees surrounded by small thorny bushes at their base. In front of him, in the middle of the field, straight ahead with just a jog to the left of the pond, was the small cage containing the prize pig. Gorry nudged Corkan on the arm and they both watched Saoi as he studied the field thinking of a strategy.

Saoi then turned to Gorry and Corkan, speaking calmly. "They may plan strategies of strength and swiftness, nevertheless, knowledge and patience will win the field today."

Finally, the battle horn sounded. Gorry scanned the field. In the near corner to his left, he watched, as one of the men ran across jagged rocks by the edge of the cliff. He tripped and fell over the uneven surface and was overtaken by an opponent; the two began to wrestle. In the far distant corner, he saw men struggling to navigate the grasses in order to reach their opponents. As each reached the other, blows were exchanged. He witnessed similar events at every corner as the men attempted to pass through obstacles, while others struggled to hold them at bay. He watched men knocking over one another; wrestling and fighting with fists until one or the other fell to the ground. Soon Gorry realized, as each man standing moved on to pursue and engage, whether in offense or defense, the man who fell to the ground, would surely rise as rapidly as able, and continue to pursue another, thus violating rule number two of the game. Gorry looked across the field, to the small white trees, where men were gathering small branches to use as clubs against each other. The same irreverence was occurring at the pond, where men cupped handfuls of mud and fashioned balls to throw, thus violating rule number three. As men were clubbed and fell to the ground, their families ran from the side to aid them and administer cloth wraps. This added to the confusion on the field and quickly turned into attacks, avenging the fallen as fathers, mothers, wives, and daughters, angered by the unfair play, stepped in to pursue the man they thought guilty, directly or by association, breaking rule number four. Chaos ensued as the relatives of those wounded gathered branches and wielded them across the head of a man, or ran to a stranger and pelted him with a ball of mud. Others joined together to hold a single man and kick him.

Fin saw the time was right, so he commanded Davison to send a group of men to circle around the backside of the pond to attack some of Greacy's men from behind. However, when they got to the end of the pond and circled around between the trees, they ran into angry family members and were held there, fighting to defend themselves. Because of the many people already fighting, the spectators began to get angry at each other and too began fighting along the edges of the field. Gorry, Corkan and Saoi remained in place, patiently watching and waiting.

When the carnage had escalated to include nearly everyone in and around the field, Gorry looked to his side and noticed Corkan and Saoi were gone. As he scanned the field straight ahead, to the left of the pond, he could see Saoi walking toward the pen, Corkan following behind. The people along the sides were so involved with the fights going on around them, no one seemed to notice the two as they arrived at the pen and meekly waited beside the gate. The Risi noticed Saoi and Corkan standing by the pen as two men from his corner of the field began to run toward them. The Risi turned from where he was and ran to catch them. When he did, he grabbed their shoulders, spun them both around and smacked their heads together, causing them to immediately drop to the ground. Saoi saw the Risi's actions and knew he had rescued him, and Corkan, from danger. The Risi stood tall as he smiled and gave his friend a nod. Saoi bowed to the Risi showing great respect and thankfulness.

The Minister had given everyone plenty of time to fight and could see the men were becoming tired. He watched as the stubborn rose again only to get a good clubbing and fall back to the earth. All around the field, men, women, and children were bleeding and sobbing. "I believe they have had enough uniting for one day," he yelled to the farmer, a man named Faragher. "I'll blow my horn. Then, you open the gate to release the pig."

The battle horn blew long and loud and the people stopped much of their fighting and looked across the field to the pen.

"Grab hold of the prize," the Minister shouted.

As the farmer raised the gate, the pig ran out of the pen and right into the waiting hands of Corkan and Saoi. At first, there was a long hush. Then, from the crowd, came a mixture of laughing, cheering, and yelling at each other. Capturing the pig happened so quickly, some didn't even realize what had occurred. The Minister, happy it was over, addressed Corkan and Saoi.

"Who are you men with?" he asked.

"Master Greacy," they answered in staggered reply.

The Minister yelled out to the crowd. "This morning, the families of Ramsey and Holmtown win the field!" Then he looked at the two again, asking, "And what be your judgement on the punishment this day?"

Saoi answered. "Let the wounds be healed. Let it be past. The whole is strengthened when stone and mortar come together."

"You are a wise man, indeed!" cried the Minister.

Not everyone cheered, nor was everyone happy about this declaration.

"The fight was not over," yelled Fin from the crowd. "You blew the horn too soon."

This enraged the Minister considerably. "Mind your tongue Fin. I am the Minister! As such I lead the game. I make the decisions."

"One day I will lead, and then I will make the decisions," shouted Fin.

As the crowd started to leave the field and return to the camp, Fin came to the side of Gorry. "You sent your hideous servants to steal the prize and take away my victory."

Greacy and several of his men moved in to hear the argument, but Gorry did not pay heed. Instead, he looked first at Saoi, then said to Fin.

"Knowledge and patience won the field today," echoing the words of Saoi.

Fin scoffed. "Have the field and your pig this day. I'll take the rest, including the heart of the fair maiden you admire from afar."

Returning to the camp for the celebration, Greacy and his men, gathered around the fire.

"God has declared us victorious men!" Greacy shouted. "Let us share our victory with all of our brothers."

The men cheered as Greacy held high a rag fixed to a long pole. In the center was a symbol, like the Sicilian banner with triskelion. Greacy had removed the image of the Gorgon and the three legs were embroidered with armor accented in gold.

"Brothers! Let us salute England, Scotland, and Ireland." He raised his skin, filled with wine, toward Davison. As Davison raised his skin, Greacy continued. "Together, we will stand like the legs of Mann. May Mann live eternal!"

Both men took a long swig then raised their skins toward the crowd. With that, all the men, except for Fin and a few of his faithful followers, roared in unity and raised their cups.

Gorry remained at the back of the crowd. Having observed the events of the day, the bloodshed of the fight, he felt even more unlike these people than when he arrived. He was disturbed by their callous actions toward one another.

They agree to one thing and do something else, whatever promotes their cause, he thought. Gorry had always believed in peace and tranquility. He was used to living quietly in his glen, being one with nature. Today he had witnessed more of the emerging evil of mankind, and his spirit was saddened. Gorry found a quiet space to lay his head, away from the celebrations of the wake, but he knew sleep would not come easy this night.

The Cherubim and the Flaming Sword

East of the Garden of Eden he stands
After God and man fall to discord
To keep the way, the tree of life
The Cherubim and his flaming sword

On the next day, the day of the funeral, the sun was just past the middle of the sky, signaling the time had arrived to start the procession through the tent for those who had come to wish the dearly departed a final farewell.

Gorry made his way to Father Druce's tent; the temporary church, which now housed the deceased. The body had been placed in an open pine coffin, and placed upon a table, where it would remain until carried to the graveyard for the service. Friends, neighbors, and fellow workers, including the Cistercian monks of Rushen Abbey and the nuns of the Douglas Priory, formed a long line, waiting to view the corpse and pay respects.

Gorry stood just inside the tent as the mourners passed through. Watching the old woman as she entered, he noticed her eyes were even more dark and sullen than before. When sufficient time had passed for all in line to give homage, the old woman slowly approached the coffin, holding the little boy by the hand. She kissed Leece gently on the brow, lovingly patting his stiff frame. She led the boy to a seat at the front of the tent by the door, quietly sobbing as the deacons secured the lid to the coffin.

Gorry saw two hooded figures standing outside the

tent seeking permission to enter. Father Druce would not allow it, saying the time for them had passed. One of the hooded men carried a sacred rod made of alder wood with ogham letters and symbols carved into it. Although they remained outside the tent, the men still tried to speak out to the dead man.

"The soul is gone away," he said to them. "Today we surrender the flesh to the earth."

As Father Druce walked toward the opening of the tent to leave for the gravesite and prepare for the service, the old woman reached out her arm to stop him.

"Leece," she said.

Father Druce stopped and looked at the woman's grief-stricken face, and into her eyes.

She spoke again. "His name was Leece."

Father Druce turned to her and spoke in a very quiet whisper. "I know his first name, Iniuria. It's just a shame no one will ever know his last."

Touching his sleeve, she said. "He has a sir name. You and I both know it."

Father Druce said nothing as he lowered his head and walked away.

The journey from the makeshift church, through the settlement and up a small hill to the graveyard, made for a long and arduous trip. Four of the closest to the deceased, fellow masons, carried the coffin at a quick pace. After a short distance, they were relieved by four others along the way and so it went until they reached the graveside. When all arrived, the coffin was lowered into the ground in a position as would allow the dead to face the sea. The old woman and little boy stood beside the dirt tomb while some of the mourners tossed small white stones into the hole believing it would ease his passage to the afterlife. Clay soil was heaped over all of it and the shovels were laid on top in the shape of a cross.

Father Druce walked over to a small mound near the grave and raised his hand. The crowd became quiet and moved in close as he spoke.

"The Lord be with you."

One of the deacons looked out on the crowd and motioned to them as if directing a choir. They responded in unison.

"And also with you."

Father Druce then lifted a vase of water.

"Dear people, this water is a symbol to remind us of our baptism, our covenant with God. Let us ask Him to bless it, to keep us faithful to his spirit. Lord God Almighty," he said looking at the sky, "hear the prayers of your people. You made the water of baptism holy by Christ's baptism in the Jordan. Through it, you give us a new birth. Bless this water which provides fruitfulness to the fields and sustains the life of man. Renew us with your Holy Spirit. We ask this through Christ our Lord."

After this, one of the deacons walked over to the mound. He was much younger than Father Druce with a very powerful, deep voice.

"The apostle Paul wrote in Romans," he began, "For

the wages of sin is death, but the gift of God is eternal life through Jesus Christ our Lord."

As the deacon continued, Gorry pondered this message, *according to that logic, if the wages of sin are death, all are guilty of sin, even the most pious, because all men die.*

As the ceremony languished, Gorry, lost in his own thoughts, was barely aware of what was being said. He vaguely heard the hymns that were sung, or scripture recited, sometimes in Greek or Latin. When he finally returned his attention to the service, Father Druce was speaking again.

"Human nature is not totally corrupt, there is good in every man. It has only been weakened and wounded by man's inclination to sin. All of mankind will continue to struggle against the persistent urges of this world. Brothers and sisters, this penchant can be reversed by baptism, which cleanses our soul and turns man back toward God. It is a choice each individual must make, either to tread the path of righteousness or go astray. I believe our good Brother Leece was on the path of righteousness and has been welcomed into heaven to join our Creator and all the virtuous souls who have gone before."

Having finished his speech, Father Druce stepped away and another deacon approached the mound. He was older and very tall and thin. He stood statuesque and spoke in a slow monotone.

"I read these words from the Gospel of Luke for you to consider as you return to your community," he said. "I say to unto you which hear, love your enemies, do good to them which hate you. Bless them who curse you. Pray for them, which despise you. For if ye love them which love you, what thank have ye? For sinners, also do even the same. Love your enemies, and do good, and lend, hoping for nothing again. Now, let us bow our heads in prayer. Holy Father we give you thanks for Bishop German. He labored to spread faith and save souls. Grant us strength like his. Give us unwavering obligation to holiness that we may build your Church and lead all people to your glory. We ask this through the intercessions of the prayers of our patron Saint German and your only son, our Lord and savior, Jesus Christ. Amen."

After the funeral, as the crowd dispersed to their homes and campsites, there were those who stayed behind and placed small stones the length of the body over the grave to mark the resting place of the dead. The smaller stones were covered with cap stones creating a cairn. Gorry watched as others, not part of the funeral procession, scavenged the ground for items of value dropped by the mourners, searching for anything they could barter with later. Still others lit small fires and danced around in, what seemed to Gorry, pagan ritual. He thought, *is this what man has become?*

Back at the church campsite, Aine was replacing apples in a dish, preparing the evening meal for her uncle and brothers. Her thoughts were wandering from one thing to the next when Father Druce came into the tent. He noticed a look of concern on her face and inquired what she was thinking.

"Uncle?" she said hesitantly, "I don't know why, but a question just came to my mind."

"What is it my dear child?"

"Uncle, do you believe there is ever a time when telling a lie is justified?"

Father Druce drew in a long, deep breath and let out a heavy sigh. "Well child, the Book of Proverbs says there are six things man shall not do, one of which is to bear false witness. You know this is one of the Commandments. What causes you to ask such a question, my innocent?"

"What of Rahab and the midwives? Was not she justified when she received the messengers and sent them out another way?"

He smiled as he placed his hand gently upon her shoulder.

"Rahab was pure of heart, she did what she believed to be right. I will tell you this, Aine, when faced with a difficult situation, like Rahab, we must carry out our actions with a pure heart. There is much evil in the world, my child. Confronted with a dire circumstance, it may be the right thing to commit a lesser sin in order to prevent a greater evil. I can think of no better justification."

Early evening dew moistened Gorry's clothes as he stood at the edge of his camp observing small groups from different beliefs act out their own religious and pagan practices, without concern for each other or the principles of the deceased. Seeing all the diverse rituals being conducted, recalling the events of the fight, and the slaughtering of pigs in celebration, he realized how little he knew of the world of man. He had often wondered why every structure built by religious organizations made to worship a trinity were erected with four sides. Today, he was reminded of all the other religions and how much their structures and philosophies differ.

"This is man," he said quietly. Then, gazing toward the heavens, he asked, "Is all this done in your image? Which gestures are holy? Which are sin? I do not understand."

I will not succumb to such an end, he thought. *What good is all this now to my dead brother? Today, I bear witness to man's fall from grace. It is all sarcasm! Nothing more. My death will not end with such mockery. These self-proclaimed men of divinity do not know the God they serve, nor do they know my world. I am here to protect it. I will wield the flaming sword and keep the way of the tree of life. I will not let them destroy Eden.*

Harmony of the Spheres

The sun, the moon, and planets share
To move in common sky from here
Celestial bodies part in collective theme
Sing in harmony of the spheres

The scent of roasted meat filled the evening air, along with muted sounds of conversations and children playing. A small group of musicians, comprised mostly of residents of the settlement, brought their instruments: a flute, a drum, a tin whistle, and a small violin. They gathered a short distance from the main tent, near Gorry, at the edge of the campsite. The fiddler scraped a worn bow across the strings, making a squeaky sound. This was followed by corresponding notes from the flute. A girl playing a tin whistle chirped the merry tune as the call was made to gather for the feast.

There was little conversation around the table as the musicians played. After each tune, a few of the seated guests would acknowledge the musicians, but for the most of it the air in the room was heavy and not everyone was happy or polite. Fin and his men were the loudest and full of wine from the start.

"The fight was not over," Fin said to Davison. "Greacy's animals should have been kept better tethered. Had anyone seen them sneak, they may have suffered a wounding blow and not be here now to watch Master Greacy celebrate. Tomorrow I lead my men out to hunt.

My men are wise as well as strong. Tomorrow, we will act like men and take our own prize in the fields and in the forests."

Greacy ignored the idle words of Fin. He rose and walked away from his table of men, and outside of the tent. There, he found the Risi, Saoi and Corkan sitting quietly on a log.

"I owe much gratitude to you," he said to Saoi and Corkan. "Your wisdom is evident; my appreciation is great. I would ask you to share in the victory at my table." He hesitated. "Well, I'm sure you understand. We are all free men, it is true. However, the people of my clan, those who rule over me and my livelihood, dictate what I am to abide by. I do hope we live to see the day when all men can sit at the same table."

"Brothers," Saoi said.

"Yes, brothers," said Greacy as he left to return to the celebration.

After the food was mostly gone and bellies were filled, the flute player blew a single note and announced the need for guests to select a mate to form couples for a dance. As he spoke, several husbands and wives, as well as others who already seemed to know whom to select, rose and formed sets.

"Kindred, neighbors, friends," he called out, "enjoy the music. Put your fears to rest. Seize the present! For if not now, then when?"

As the music began, the couples patterned their dance into figures full of graceful movements, in a gentle, easy-flowing style. The dancers changed partners throughout, always focusing upon one another as they danced the various patterns. Aine had not chosen a partner, wishing for Gorry to choose her. When he did not, she made her way around the outside of the crowd to stand next to him. She stepped sideways, slowly coming closer.

"Would you care to join me and step in?" she asked when finally arriving at his side.

Gorry's body gave a jerk. She had caught him unaware. He looked at her oval face, with its fair features, and her soft smooth hair, without saying a word.

Finally, Gorry gathered his courage and said, "Your offer is a polite gesture, indeed. Forgive me, fair one. However, I prefer to simply observe. I am not much good at the dance."

"Don't be nervous. It is easy to learn."

"I understand the individual movements. It is the meaning of the dance in whole I fail to understand."

"Music and dance are essential in modern society. It promotes a sense of harmony of spirit."

"I understand the perceived benefits. But, these dances are nothing more than people forming squares, circles and triangles. It is only a manipulation and ordering, or reordering, of patterns, of geometric shapes. These are the same patterns I see in nature, in the hills, the glens, the forests, and the gardens. I don't need to recreate them with dance. This is nothing more than a performance, a dance of the muses, to imitate relationships." Suddenly embarrassed, wishing he would have just accepted her invitation, but also, not knowing what to say next, Gorry awkwardly excused himself and walked away.

Aine's heart ached with disappointment wishing he understood the greater benefits of participating in the common ritual.

Outside the circle of the crowd, just beyond the light of the campfire, Gorry saw a small boy crumpled beside a hitching post. He could see him twisting and turning, struggling. He ran to his side and could see the straps of a harness were wrapped around the boy's neck and bound tightly. Each time the boy pulled, in an effort to escape, the straps tightened. Gorry swiftly lifted the boy with one hand and untied the straps with his other. The boy took a deep breath, gasping, grabbing hold of the post. He held to it firmly staring with glazed eyes into the light and the shadows of people dancing.

"How did this happen?" asked Gorry. "What are you doing here?"

"I wandered away from my grandmother so she would not see me cry. My father was buried today and I have no mother," the boy said looking past Gorry, into the darkness.

Gorry then realized who the boy was. "Fear not, child."

"I have no fear, sir. I feel only great sorrow."

"You are too young to have such a broken heart."

Just then the old woman came around from behind the tent franticly searching for the boy. She rushed over to them. "I am his grandmother," she said, looking only at the boy.

"He is a brave one," Gorry said to the old woman. Then, he leaned over and spoke to the boy, "What is your name?"

"Justus. My father called me Justus."

"Well, Justus, be patient and know your god is near. He will protect you. I am sorry you have suffered this evil. I wish you well and may God be with you."

Gorry returned to his campsite, where the men were still drinking, celebrating, and gloating over their victory on the field. Talk of the dead man, Leece, had ceased the moment he was in the ground. The sun slowly dropped beyond the horizon and the sky became dark. The day had come to an end and people were beginning to prepare for slumber in the chilly night air. Gorry looked across the darkness, to the fire of the Risi, Corkan and Saoi, where the men sat quietly. He grabbed a flaming stick from the fire and walked across the field to the edge of their camp.

"May I join you?" he asked.

"Why?" asked Corkan.

"I wanted to commend you for catching the pig yesterday," he said. "Well done."

"Thank you," replied Corkan.

"Come near to our fire and be warm," Saoi said.

Gorry stepped into the ring of trampled, matted grass and sat beside the Risi. "You are Saoi," Gorry said, acknowledging him. "And you are Corkan." Each of the men nodded as he spoke. Then, Gorry turned to the Risi and asked, "Why do men call you the Risi? Is this the name you go by?"

His bold inquiry of the giant made Saoi and Corkan nervous, for no one ever spoke directly to him, especially asking him a question of such personal nature. The Risi could sense their emotions, so he raised his hand to calm them.

"Come gather round, my friends," he said in a deep velvet baritone. "I will tell you of the Risi." He leaned in close to the fire. "I will tell you of a man called Iniko, an African prince who deeply loved and wanted to marry a beautiful maiden called Folami. Iniko's grandfather, the king, would not give his blessing for the two to be wed. To keep Folami away from Iniko, the king sold her as a slave and she was taken to a faraway land.

"One day, sometime later, a ship arrived at Prince Iniko's shore. The captain invited Iniko and his men to come aboard for a meal and drinks. After filling the men with much wine, the captain took Iniko and his men prisoners and set sail in the dark of night.

"When the ship arrived at a foreign harbor, Prince Iniko was renamed to Caesar. He was sold to a man named Trefry who soon came to like and admire the prince. In time, Caesar found out Folami was a slave on the same plantation; but, her name had been changed to Kirabo.

"After many months, Caesar and Kirabo found each other and rekindled their passion. Shortly after that Kirabo realized she was pregnant. Caesar tried to free his family, because he did not want his children born into slavery. Even though Trefry was fond of Caesar, he would not allow him to go free. In desperation, Caesar tried to lead the slaves in a revolt, but he was betrayed, caught, and badly beaten.

"He and his wife with child did eventually escape the plantation on their own and secretly boarded a ship. He was once again Prince Iniko and she, Princess Folami. He would take his Folami to a distant land where they could be safe, live free and raise their child.

"Only one day, when the child was newly born, while they were still on the ship at sea, a great wind increased. Thunder and lightning flashed while heavy rain pounded the waves. The raging waters tossed the ship back and forth until it struck some large rocks along the seashore. The ship sank along the coast just south of this place. The sea tried to take Iniko's wife and newborn child, but their souls rose and floated into the sky."

Iniko paused and took a deep breath. "Iniko knew your Fides," he said turning his head to face Gorry. "Fides was a very strong man, a very spiritual man. He found me on the shore, helped me find food, clothing, and a home. Your Fides always showed respect to Iniko. He was the only man on this Island who called me by my given name."

When Iniko finished, the men sat silently staring into the fire, watching the flames flicker. After some time, Gorry rose to go back to his campsite for the night.

"Thank you, Iniko, I feel you are now my brother. Sleep well my friends." Gorry said as he left the three men.

A Song for Mona

The beautiful lily of the pond

Once again at the campsite Gorry had joined upon his arrival, he huddled close to the fire for warmth. Having much on his mind and unable to settle, he pulled out a quill, some ink and parchment, and by the glow of the fire began to write:

I dreamed a dream a fortnight ago
That life is a rhyme I did not know
Each verse wrote itself, revealing to me
I'm part of the whole of life's harmony

In the days before time, in the heavens I dined
Within a garden which billowing clouds did line
There I chanced upon a sacred pond and did see
In the middle, all alone, a beautiful lily

The most beautiful of all, so to the gods I did plea
When time would permit, there would they place me?
When the time had come, to the earth green and blue
Your beauty shared with me, and I with you

The sea softly breathed, singing a gentle sigh
Our souls entwined as time passed by
A melody of love played upon the lyre
Consuming my mind with a love so rare

A sweet melody plays an unwritten song
As the blended score of our love doth play on
I think of you each morning as I kiss the dew
I crave your sweet nectar, my mouth longs for you

Each day I awake, and gaze upon your scene
Your gentle rolling hills pristine
The shadows made fresh from a sun that climbs
Fades quickly to brightness with hastening time

Life reveals a rainbow, its unending hues
Within your valley, moist with morning dew
And all the songs birds sing their tune
Inspired by your beauty; lovely and true

Untouched by man, his repugnant ways
You fostered me 'tween your hills and bays
Spring did not last as we had desired
Taken by summer, as fate does require

Long was the sun on our juvenile pleasure
Seduced by the light and desired without measure
When I lay upon you, the soul of earth I do feel
I lust for your charms, to my heart they appeal

Oh, to be master of all surrounding you
The mist, the waters, and sky of deep blue
My arms reach around you, all embracing
Summer memories fade, as time is racing

If all I am meant to be is a reflection of you
To be a part of your perfect self, as nature can do
To walk with you always along the shores of the sea
I am completed by you, for you define me.

And when I grow old and feeble and lame
I will love you eternal and worship the same
Please know I am loyal to your innocence and grace
And my life was well lived to the end on this place

Given the chance and the zeal, I swear
Your dignity, my coat of armor I bear
I Soldier on into darkness without fright
In the final battle in the cold winter night

The tarries and toils of time past I fear
The darkness prevails, the sun doth disappear
Death escorts down the lonely path to the door
Where we must enter, bound to pass through no more

In the days before time, in the heavens I dined
Within a garden which billowing clouds did line
There I chanced upon a sacred pond and did see
In the middle, all alone, a beautiful lily

After he had completed writing, Gorry placed the quill and ink back into his pouch. He folded the small piece of parchment and held it close to his chest. As the fires grew dim and the sounds of men faded, he fell into a deep sleep.

A Sickle, A Raven, and A Crown

So wields the weapon of time and fate
The crier of death warns of justice devised
Caution the word to those who listen
A sickle, a raven, and a crown to the wise

Roused from slumber by hushed whispers all around him, and the scuffle of men, horses, and dogs, Gorry opened his eyes. The moon had not yet given way to the sun as Fin and a great number of men prepared to go on a hunt. They had assembled several bundles of skins some containing water, some wine, along with cooking pots, and sacks full of bread, flint, and other items they would need. The bags and pots were tied tightly on two long sticks strapped together and fashioned to fit over a man's shoulders and be dragged along behind. The skins were divided evenly and strapped to each man's horse. Gorry shivered from the briskness of the pre-dawn hour. Pulling an extra skin around his shoulders he leaned in to stoke the fire.

"Better a slaughter in the country than the month of March should come in mild," Fin said as he approached.

Gorry knew the meaning of this phrase, however, the ways of old were strict regarding hunting, including what should be hunted and when.

"During this season, our dominion over the pasture is as a shepherd," Gorry cautioned. "To hunt out of season, to strike the innocent early, is callous."

"Will you join us?" Fin asked. "Put aside our differences and enjoy our human dominance over nature."

"Were the season right, I would join you," replied Gorry. "Today, I beg you wait until the time is proper. Let the young lambs and fawns grow to maturity, do not slaughter the innocent."

"My men and I will wait no longer," said Fin. "To the south and west we ride on this land, past the well of wisdom, to the edge of the mountains. We travel to the head of your glen in search of magic mead. We wish to taste the ale so age, nor sickness, nor death can touch us."

"Like those before you," Gorry warned, "you will learn The Red Man appears in many forms."

"Oh yes," jeered Fin. "And as for you, beware your cousin, the buggane!" Saying this, he walked up and down the ranks, commanding the men to follow him and hunt well. As Fin passed by one last time, Gorry could see the glittering of arrows in his pack. They were made by Fin's own hand to be sleek, with a slender shaft, each with a distinguishable carving along the stone tip.

Those burdened with dragging the supplies started out. They would set up tents and make camp at the base of the hill on farmer Faragher's field and wait for Fin and the others to join them on their return from the hunt.

Aine's brothers were among the men on horseback who would join in the hunt.

"Bode well this day, for you will be protected by the women and small children," her older brother said to Gorry as he rode by. "Only the men shall hunt today," he scoffed.

Gorry could see Aine standing across the way, so he said nothing in reply.

Then, her brother looked over at her, pointing to Gorry. "See your man now? He is different from civilized men. Why doesn't he just return to his Eden?"

Her brother's words were so unkind, Aine thought, and she was embarrassed for both herself and Gorry. Not knowing what to do, she returned to Father Druce's tent to help prepare the morning meal.

Fin, his son, Oshin, and many men traveled south heading to lands along the edge of the mountain, taking with them scores of bandogs. They left behind at the settlement travelers, beggars, priests, Corkan, Saoi, and Gorry. They also left behind wives and children, including Fin and Oshin's daughters and all the young maidens. Like her father, Fin's daughter respected no one. She and her friends were always plotting some mischief, especially when her father was gone. They were known to perform acts so wild, they often provoked chastisement and rebuke.

After Fin and his men left, Gorry decided to rest a while longer. It was still early in the day and he knew he only had half a day's walk ahead of him to get safely back to the glen by dark. Gorry settled closer to the warm fire and pulled the skin tight around him.

When his eyes were finally sealed by a deep slumber, Fin's daughter gathered a few of the maidens and whispered to them. "Gather round my pretties and tell me how this man shall be tested?"

The maidens did not understand.

Fin's daughter continued. "See young Gorry lying over there, by the fire?" she asked. "I think he is much too light as a man. The others know my father is a wise leader and have gone with him to hunt."

Still, the girls looked at her confused.

So, she explained, "For him to show disloyalty to such a wise and great leader is treachery and should not be tolerated. He must be taught a lesson."

Now, Oshin's daughter mischievously joined in the scheme. She commanded, "Hurry my young lambs, gather some rope and bring it to us hastily."

Doing as they were told, the girls went around the campsite, looking until they found some sturdy rope.

"Come with me," said Fin's daughter. "We will punish this fool who refuses my father's, all of our fathers', fellowship. Let us teach him a lesson or two."

Oshin's daughter commanded, "Go tie this end fast to the harrow there, and tie this end to his mane."

The girls hastily followed her orders, cautiously laying the rope as taut as could be, securing each end so it could not easily be undone. Using more rope, they secured his feet to one of the logs used for seating. Then, Oshin's daughter gently kicked a burning ember from the fire until it touched the bottoms of Gorry's feet. The girls ran and hid beside a tent, crouching behind a few barrels, to witness the embarrassment. Fin and Oshin's daughters did not run. They did not hide, as the others. Instead, they stayed a short distance away. Fin's daughter stood with hands clenched into fists, resting them upon the sides of her waist as she watched.

Gorry awoke startled and in great pain. He tried to sit, but as he rose, the rope tied to his hair seized tightly and would not let him. He also could not move his feet, as they were secured to the log. He fell back to the ground, perplexed, howling with frustration and pain. The girls laughed as he tried to free himself a second and third time. Some villagers standing a short distance away saw Gorry struggling and heard the girls laughing, but they were unaware of his dilemma. They had not seen the girls plot this revenge and thought it merely a jest, some sort of glib performance. Soon, there were many spectators, all unaware of his burning feet, all taunting him as if participating in a sarcasm. Several more times Gorry tried to free himself and draw away from the burning embers.

"That will teach you to dishonor my father!" Fin's daughter shouted, as she and all the maidens ran away to the village.

"Finally understanding the situation, some of those standing near to him started over to see what they could do. Corkan and Saoi had heard the growing uproar and ran over to him fast to untie him and cool his feet with a sack of water.

"Here, drink some. I will pour the rest on your blistered heels," said Corkan. "We were busy with camp when we heard the commotion. Those wretched girls."

As the confused villagers dispersed and returned to

their work Corkan and Saoi stayed a while, helping Gorry wrap his feet.

"They have gone too far," Corkan said. "Something must be done."

"It goes on without regard," added Saoi. "Each generation degrades from the base deeds of the previous."

Gorry rose with much pain in his feet, and even greater pain in his heart. The words of his companions were unsettling and true, he felt. *Each generation degrades until they have gone too far. The pendulous morality of this village must be brought to center. The deeds need to be countered, the wrongs made right.*

"Fin and Oshin's daughters', and their sprites', actions must be named," Gorry said in a quiet monotone. "The culprits of this harrying will someday receive due recognition for their conduct."

Morning shadows had disappeared when Gorry said his goodbyes to the Risi, Corkan, and Saoi and set out to return to his haven. He held a long, narrow stick tightly, to aid him as he walked across the pathway to the top of the hill. Gorry began to feel faint as he maneuvered around rocks and snags and his mind wandered. He thought of all the people he had met, and events witnessed. He struggled to understand why all this merriment was considered morally accepted at a time when people should be contemplating their own actions, consequences, and demise. His feet aching, Gorry sat for a while on a small, flat stone below the branches of a tree. He looked to the east, at the majestic mountains, memorized by their glory. He inhaled the sweet aroma of life all around him, admiring the new buds on the trees, and new growth on plants springing from the ground. He listened to the loud chirping sounds of the sacred wren. Along the hedgerow beside where he sat, Gorry saw a patch of plants with bright yellow flowers. Some of the flowers were surrounded by purple colored berries. He believed they were bullace, so he pulled several berries off the plant, filling his hand and a small pouch in is pack.

As Gorry ate a handful of the berries, his focus began to blur. The plants with bright yellow flowers swayed before him. Rubbing his eyes, he looked across the valley at the settlement and the ground below it, both appearing to be sliding away from him. Strange illusions tricked his mind. He heard the rustling of tall grass being sifted through by something or someone approaching. Dizzy and disoriented, he tried to stand. As he rose, a glashtin unexpectedly appeared before him.

"Why are you so far from the stream," he said to the disfigured goblin.

"I must share with you my vision," the glashtin replied.

"Have you come all the way from my glen?"

"This land, your garden, is in danger of being disturbed from the falls of the glen to the mountains." The glashtin spoke with great movement of his hands, his fingers bent and twisted. "The shrill of our sacred bird warns of it. A spirit who is sovereign will join the dead soon and the Moon Goddess delights."

"Have you seen this?"

"No, the wren, who is supreme among all birds, told me of this prophecy."

"Go on," begged Gorry.

"Three symbols it saw in its mind and shared with me: A harvesting sickle, a raven, and a crown."

"What do the symbols mean?"

"The first is Cronos, the second is Bran, and the third is Arthur. These represent time, protection, and martyrdom."

"What is the prophecy?"

"Protection from the goddess of earth, fire, and fertility, Nantosuelta, will be weakened over time. Blood runs from the tip of Nantosuelta's rod. It is the blood of an archer, a skilled warrior, who hunts the innocent with slender arrow. When the innocent approach the archer, the sacred bird will nip his ear and thus reveal his presence so the innocent may flee entrapment."

"I must think upon your prophecy and its meaning."

"That is not all," he continued. "Not all of the innocent will be able to flee. Many will die at the assail of the archer, upsetting the balance of the land. That is the message."

Remembering the tradition of giving the glashtin something of value in return for his vision, Gorry looked in his pack to find something to offer him. Retrieving one of the pelts he had brought with him he looked up to hand it to the goblin, but the creature had vanished.

With an uneasy mind, Gorry stumbled over the top of the grassy hill and went south until he came upon the sacred woods he had avoided on his way north. The day was warmer than usual and his feet throbbed angrily, so Gorry decided to take a shorter path this time, crossing directly through the grove. The tall trees were surrounded at their base by a sea of vines, with thorns and brush so thick only a hare could travel with some ease. Gorry soon became tired of pushing back the shoots and branches, held in place by thick canes. His arms and hands were scratched and dotted with blood. Midway through the woods, he came to a good resting place, so he sat for a moment on a small mound of earth and ate more berries for nourishment.

"Spirit," he whispered to the sky. "Again, I call you to come hither and be with me this day. Be my guide as I travel this road alone. Stop the hunters and spare the innocent." A cool breeze blew through the grove. Gorry closed his eyes and sighed deeply, wishing he were already safely back in his glen, cooling his feet in the brook.

A rustling in the ground cover and a snort like that of a hog startled him. He opened his eyes and saw a glimpse of another being, a hairy little man, disappearing behind a tree.

"Come present," Gorry called out from his perch. "Fear not. Make yourself known," he said in slurred speech. A small hideous man covered from head to toe in thick, bushy, black hair, came out from behind the tree. His eyes were bright, like flaming torches.

"What are you?" Gorry asked, unafraid.

The creature did not answer.

"I ask you again! Man, or beast?"

Still, the being did not reply.

"Well, I must move on," Gorry said, staggering toward the man beast. "Move from my way or be pushed aside."

Then the hairy being's eyes pooled with water, the torches dulled, as he spoke in a sad, gravelly voice.

"They call me buggane. The fair people of the glen asked me to seek you."

"The An Domhain?" Gorry asked.

The creature nodded slowly, first staring at Gorry for a moment, then looking toward the sky. "Man has despised the commandment of the Lord and committed evil in his sight. Behold, look how they have scarred this land, ignored the seasons. Therefore, there will be no peace night or day."

After he said this, the buggane's eyes returned to their brilliant light, so much so that Gorry raised his arm to shield his eyes from the blinding illumination. When the brightness disappeared, he lowered his arm and the buggane was gone.

Not far away, at the base of the mountain gently sloping toward the peak in the east, Fin and his men were hunting. They were even fiercer in hunting than they were in battle. Fin felt if he took a man's life, he must account for his soul. If he took the life of an animal, he was merely demonstrating superiority over creation. The entire world, he believed, belonged to man for his enjoyment.

Two local farmers, Forsdal and Faragher, had agreed to let the men hunt and camp on their land so long as they cleared away all they brought with them, or killed. They did not want predators to smell blood or food and be drawn to their chickens and sheep.

Out on the green meadow, Fin saw what appeared to be a gray fawn running across the plain. He called to his men to set after the fawn. Near as they kept to her, he kept nearer to them, until at last they reached the stream which flowed from the mountain, cutting its way through the glen, splitting the soil and rocks and forest on its way to the sea. They were no sooner at the stream when the fawn vanished. They did not know in which direction it had gone, so Fin and his men separated. Fin went westward and followed the water into the glen. His men rode toward the east along the mountain slopes.

It was not long until Fin had entered a part of the forest filled with haze so dense he could not see far in front of him. He dismounted his horse, tied it to a tree and traveled on through the forest by foot. The ground was uneven, and the fog so thick, he tripped and struck his head on the surface of a large rock, causing him to sleep for a moment. When he awoke, he thought he heard muffled sounds of people nearby. They were talking in an incoherent language, discussing something in dreadful tones, so he hiked in their direction to see if they might help him find the fawn. Unexpectedly, before him, sitting on a rock at the water's edge, was a young woman. She was completely bare, covered only by her own garnet hair flowing from her head, wrapping loosely around her like a robe. She was the most beautiful woman he had ever seen, having skin as white as a lily, and eyes like the stars in time of frost. She seemed to be in some way sorrowful, despondent. Fin asked her if she had seen the fawn pass by.

"I did not see," she said, "and it is little I am thinking of your fawn, or your hunting, but the cause of my own trouble."

"What ails you, fairest nymph with skin like fresh milk?" asked Fin. "Is there any help I can give you? Any assistance I can offer? Whatever you wish, I will take as my command."

"This day the handsome pursuer does not consider his fate? Does he think he is entitled reprieve from the lady of this land?"

Fin, mesmerized by her beauty, offered again. "Without knowledge of your meaning, to obtain your appreciation, tell me what you seek and I will find it."

"Very well," said the woman. "A red stone, like the color of my hair, has fallen from its setting, into the pond. Will you bring it back to me?"

Fin agreed, took off his clothes and went into the pond nestled beside the flowing stream. Three times he entered. Three times he walked back and forth in the pond searching for the desired object. On the third try, he found the stone and stood, raising the prize. He looked around the pond in every direction, however, the beautiful woman had vanished.

When Fin came to the bank of the pond, he could not so much as reach to where his clothes were. For he, the mighty warrior, hunter, and leader of men, had transformed into a gray old man, weak and withered from the touch of this magical stone. Presently, his men came into the glen and happened upon him. They did not recognize him in his withered form, so they continued on, searching for both fawn and master. Weary from the search, they made their way back to the campsite at the base of the mountain on the farmer's lands.

Upon their arrival, one of the men asked, "Where is Fin?"

No one knew where he had gone. Concerned, the chief men of the party mounted their horses and rode back out to look for him, to know his condition before the sunset. They headed swiftly back toward the glen. As they approached the forest they saw Fin's horse tied to a tree. Passing through the fog-covered ground they came to the pond. There they saw the withered old man again sitting beside the water and thought him to be a spirit.

"Tell us, Spirit, did you see a gray fawn go by with a tall fair-haired man chasing after her?" one of his men queried.

"I did think the fawn entered the forest," said Fin with a weak and shaky voice, "but I do not remember the man."

"Tell us, where are they presently, Spirit," commanded another of his men.

Fin made no answer, for he had not the courage to say to them that he himself was their mighty leader. For in his present condition, he was unable to leap, run, or even walk without stooping.

One of the chiefs took out his sword from its sheath

and commanded, "Speak promptly old man. It is short till you will have the knowledge of death unless you tell us what you know."

Reluctantly, still fearing they would not believe him, Fin told them the whole story. When the men heard, and knew it was him, they cried out. The men asked if there was any cure to be found.

"There is," he said. "I know well this enchantment was put upon me by a daughter of the fair people. Take me to the edge of the glen, to the waterfall. There I will find the Spirit of Man and I will beg him for my shape again."

Fin's men raised him gently upon their shoulders, carrying him along the path to the falls. There they found the Spirit of Man, who came out from behind the wall of gushing water, holding in his hand a vessel of gold decorated with red stones.

"Who gave you this curse?" asked the Spirit.

"A woman. One of the An Domhain, surely," said Fin.

"How odd," said the Spirit. "They would place no such curse for they are pure of heart." Then he said, "Describe her to me. What did she say?"

Fin thought for a moment, then said, "She called herself the lady of this land."

The Spirit reared his head until his whole body was erect. "You were cursed by the lady of the land?"

"Yes," answered Fin. "Be not perplexing and tell us what you understand."

Fin and his men listened carefully as he explained. "The lady of the land is, indeed, the land," he said, his eyes brimming with tears. "You have brought offense to her. I should not reverse her decision to shame you."

Fin begged, saying, "I have learned my lesson, Spirit. If I may be restored to my old self I will protect the land."

The Spirit did not know if he believed Fin, but erring on the side of compassion, he said, "I will take the side of forgiveness this day, however, I will leave a mark upon you so you will always remember your actions. Drink this," he said handing the vessel to Fin.

No sooner did Fin drink than his whole shape and strength came back to him. When he had drunk every last drop in the vessel, it slipped from his hand falling to the earth, vanishing before it touched the ground. When Fin looked up, the Spirit of Man was gone. Fin's crown of once-yellow hair, from that day forward, remained gray because he had offended the lady of the land, who had been named Mona by the kings of the ancient world.

With the sun sinking low, Fin and his men returned to the campsite very fatigued and famished. The men had spent much of the day searching for Fin and little on hunting, catching nothing.

"Shame we should starve while the lambs get fat from the grasses," said one of the men.

"Too bad we can't eat the grasses," said another.

The complaining went on until finally, Fin commanded the men to take enough lambs for the whole camp. "Their flesh is tender and sweet," he told one of the chiefs. "Dress them in the field, then bring their meat to the fires on a stick. I will repay the farmer tomorrow."

Fin's men went out into the field to catch and kill the innocent suckling lambs, including two who had strayed from their mother's side. Drinking from a skin filled with wine, while watching his men, Fin's lustful desire for hunting returned. He saw great sport in this, so he and a few of his men decided to make torches, go back out and come around the field from the other side to see what else they may take.

Fin said to his men, "Take all you desire. Believe me, for I speak the truth. There is and always will be plenty boaghans, purrs, and the beardies. They flourish on this isle, and will be here always."

As Fin and the men set out, they came upon a stray lamb jumping and playing in the tall grass. They crouched low to the ground so the lamb could not see them as they approached. All of the sudden, a tiny wren swooped in and pinched Fin's ear with his beak. Fin let out a howl, which revealed his presence, and the lamb ran away.

"Little witch!" Fin cried out at the bird, as his men laughed. To avenge the bird's attack, Fin ordered the men to find the nest and steal the eggs within.

The men were afraid because they had heard many sayings, all of which were bad, so they said to him, "Please, my lord, it is not good we do this thing. To do so would condemn our homes and our families in the settlement."

"I will have my revenge against this witch, for I know she only disguises herself as a wren," said Fin, picking up his bow and arrows from the ground and running in the direction the wren flew.

When Fin and his men finally returned to the campsite, they were accosted by the angry farmer. "I shared my lands with you so you and your men could settle peacefully!" cried the farmer to Fin. "You repay me by taking my young lambs. Look at your gray hair, you have angered the gods."

"Hush, Uncle," Fin replied. "I lead here. I will make the decisions."

"You cannot will yourself power over the gods, nor the mother of nature," the farmer said. "I fear you have strayed, Fin. I only pray you have not wakened the Dullahan!"

"Enough of this, Uncle! I've had a long enough day," said Fin. "Let us alone to settle this night and I will have my men provide you adequate recompense tomorrow."

Gorry rested for a while considering all things that had been revealed to him by the glashtin and the buggane. When he had regained some of his strength, he decided to continue home. Exiting the woods, he chose to walk toward the highlands, since the land was rolling, less rugged, and might be softer on his charred feet. From there, he would enter the glen from the east where the river made its way through his forest, flowing to the sea. Gorry's return home had taken much longer than he anticipated and soon the afternoon sky had turned to dark gray. Along his path he came upon the fields of the farmers. He could see the glow of the fires from the campsite where Fin and his men were feasting in merriment. He could see the farmer walking across the meadow to the men, but was not close enough to know the conversation. Feeling fatigued and lightheaded, Gorry sat at the base of a shade tree and ate a few more of the berries.

That same evening, back at the settlement, Aine watched as beggars plundered vacated campsites, looking for anything of value. She saw a woman holding a piece of parchment, examining it with an odd expression. Thinking it of no value to her, the woman came over to Aine.

"This has markings on it: some kind of writing. I was never taught to read," she said handing it to Aine.

"Let me see," said Aine. She took the parchment from the woman's hand. As Aine began to read what was written, tears swelled in her eyes.

"Are you all right, miss?" asked the woman.

"Yes," replied Aine. As she thought to herself, *what man is this who is so devoted, so kind and loving?*

When she had finished reading the entire poem she asked the woman exactly where she had found it. When the woman pointed directly to where Gorry had slept by the fire, Aine was dismayed.

My heart is heavy and my pride suffers, she thought. *He may proclaim his love for her, however, I will not despair, for it may be only a fleeting desire. No, I will be patient and wait. One day, he will notice my affection for him, understand who I am. Then, I will detach him from this whimsy. I will make him faithful and loyal to me. I will cause him to desire me more than he does her.* Aine placed the folded piece of parchment into her pocket and walked back to her campsite.

Weary from the day, Aine returned to her tent directly after her evening meal with Father Druce. There she found her brother, the younger kinder one, who had not spoken rudely to Gorry. He had returned early being disappointed with the hunt and not wishing to spend the night in the farmer's pasture.

Aine, being curious about the woman named in the poem, asked him, "Do you know a girl called Mona?"

Her brother let out a chuckle.

Aine became embarrassed and asked again, "Brother, do you know of her? A girl named Mona? You must tell!"

Her brother answered, "Ah, you are an innocent one indeed, sister. All men know of Mona." He chuckled again.

Aine was beginning to feel angry, so she asked a third time, "What makes you laugh? Do you know Mona? Tell me."

"Mona is not a girl, foolish child. Mona is Man. She is us; and we are hers."

"Brother, don't speak in riddles," Aine raised her voice.

"Calm down, young one. Mona was the name of our land long before it was called Man. Now settle down and go to bed."

Aine retired to her corner of the tent. Settling in under a cover of warm blankets, she fell soundly asleep. Almost immediately, her mind was occupied by a dream. Aine imagined she was walking around, across the rivulet where all sorts of festivities were taking place. In her fantasy, she was surrounded by colorful tents and entertainers. Approaching a large dark building, she felt herself pass through the walls and found herself standing alone just inside. Impish creatures encircled the space within, guarding the darkness like an army. This place was familiar to her. She remembered accidently going into a structure much like this when she was a small girl. All around her she saw strange characters. A man with a tall hat stood in the center. He wore brightly-colored clothing. Beings, part human and part cattle danced about. One of them, a man with horns, broke from the crowd and chased a girl, who was partially covered with an animal hide. When he caught her, he laid upon her and she cried out. Afraid, Aine tried to call out for help. She saw the man in horns look at her, she tried to run, to hide from this evil she did not understand. She saw herself trying to escape through the outer wall of the building as the man ran toward her, but she could not move. Just before he reached her, the images disappeared into blackness. Aine stirred in her bed. She did not know the meaning of this vision. It felt real, like a memory. Aine supposed it to be only her imagination.

This time, as she settled in again, drifting off, her thoughts took her to another place: a safe place. A different fantasy, in which she imagined the sounds of splashing water nearby. As she came closer to the sound, she could see her childhood friends bathing in a pool of water. Aine joined them and they splashed and laughed, recalling a time of innocence; a time when the world was a place to play and there were no thoughts of wrong. In her dream, she looked away from her friends to a flowing stream cascading from the mountain, through a wooded glen, out to the sea. When she turned her gaze back to the pond, her friends had disappeared. She sat alone, the cool water caressing her bare skin.

This vision swiftly faded and she now saw herself standing in a vast meadow of soft, green grass drawing with her hand, as if she were painting. She followed her hand as it drew around two small, rounded hills above a narrow valley, which led to a small, shallow pool. Her hand moved softly beyond the pool, where a thin grove of lush shrub lay. In her dream she saw, in the distance, a man with long dark hair, mounted upon a great horse. She admired his longsword, unsheathed, laying across his lap. The man and the horse did not see her, but instead strode gracefully and gallantly to the other side of the meadow. She called out to him repeatedly, until he took notice of her and rode to her side. He lifted her onto his saddle and she felt an invigorating sensation surge through her, for she had never ridden a horse before. In her dream, she rode unafraid and held on to the man's waist until they arrived at the other end of the field. There, they dismounted, underneath the shade of a large tree. When he lifted her off the saddle, she leaned in and kissed him and he kissed her. Near the base of the tree, they lay on the ground, gently caressing each other. *Take me,* she felt herself saying, *and let me be with you.* However, this gallant gentleman only smiled at her, and said nothing. *I would leave all I have and run away with you,* she imagined herself telling him. The man gently touched her eyes causing them to close. When she opened them again she found, placed beside her, a bouquet of green nettle leaves with a single yellow flower in the middle. The mysterious stranger was gone.

Aine awoke, thinking of the yellow flower, longing to know more about the man in the dream. She felt she had dreamt some part of this before, but did not understand its meaning. Lying there in stillness of the night she let out a wistful sigh.

As Gorry listened to the revelry of Fin and his men from under the shade tree, he watched as Fin's men circled the farmer, taunting, and mocking him. He thought, *How far will man go in conquest, plundering, and stealing for his own desires? These criminals take more than simple possessions for sustenance. They take away the livelihood and freedom of others.* Then he smelled something foul nearby and could hear flies buzzing. As he surveyed the land, he could see bones and entrails of several lambs strewn across the open field.

After a moment, Gorry sensed the presence of a dog. It was smooth-haired, and measured as high as his waist. Its black, gray, and tan fur was so intimately mixed it was hard to determine the true color.

"Are you here to fight me over bones and intestines?" Gorry spoke aloud to the dog. "Can you speak as I imagine? Are you real? Hear me, my good guardian! It was not I who took the life of these innocent creatures."

The dog held his place. He wagged his tail to show he was both friendly and dignified.

"Ah, I see," Gorry said, patting the dog on his head. "You are the farmer's dog. You saw what these men did. They have rendered your service useless by their callousness. The liberties these men take are not without consequences. Manannan is my father, Mona my mother."

Observing the gluttonous men across the field, Gorry said, "I must take a stand against those who choose to violate nature by their own selfish desires. I will not stand beside the field any longer."

The sky turned to black while Gorry ate the last of the berries. Feeling his senses deceiving him, distorting his vision, he let out an earnest sigh, he would not make it home to his glen this night so he made camp under the shade tree on a bed of soft leaves. The dog would not leave him, so the two curled up side by side, each keeping the other warm.

King of Man: God of Mankind

Earthly kingdoms men divide
Those of conquest seek to find
Pleasures of power fall quickly with time
For none is greater than God of Mankind

As nature's hums quieted, Gorry began to recall his travels. He considered the innocence of the An Domain, and of Prettanike upon his throne, admiring his progeny. He remembered the wisdom of Saoi, Corkan and the Risi, three strangers who had befriended him. He thought of all the rituals performed at the wake and the cruel prank played on him that morning by Fin and Oshin's daughters. Then the warnings from the glashtin and the buggane came to mind. As Gorry's reality gave way to his subconscious he imagined the villagers had taken up weapons, following Fin and his men to the glen to conquer the fair people and the Spirit of Man. The faces of the men from the settlement were strange though: charred black. All the men carried thin shovels and torches, which burned brightly like the sun. Behind them, their women cried while the children stood emotionless and solemn. The men brought other tools Gorry did not recognize, large tools used for digging, with small carts not made of wood. In this dream Gorry whispered, "Spirit, come hither and be with me. These images are strange; how shall I understand them?"

"It is not your destiny," a soft voice murmured. "It is

of the future. There will be more men, like Fin, who come to Mona, stealing precious minerals from her mighty bosom. Many will prosper, while others will become weak and succumb to an early grave."

"Why do these people come to my glen?" he asked, but there was no answer.

In his deepest sleep, Gorry dreamt he was a young druid, out by himself in the countryside in search of hidden wisdom. In this state of being, he imagined he stumbled upon a wren, which gave him joy at first, thinking he would be blessed with great knowledge of finding the elusive divinity within all life. At this, he was satisfied and content, until he found that the wren's nest was empty, the shells broken, lying fractured on the ground.

Then he envisioned the carcasses of the innocent lambs that had been slaughtered. Overtaken by despair, Gorry cradled his face in his hands. Upon closer observation he could see an arrow. Upon the shaft of the arrow was mounted a stone tip, with a distinguishable carving. At last, he saw an image of the farmer, Faragher, hung by his neck from a tree branch. His eyes were wide-open staring at Gorry.

"You are master now," said the hanging man. "You are master and you must defend this destruction."

Gorry began to tremble.

"You are master," the farmer said in a weaker voice. "Mona calls you!" Then he gave up the ghost.

Gorry awoke feeling disturbed and disoriented. Broken memories returned to him: Walking along the edge of the farmer's field, hearing the distant revelry of Fin and his men, the plea of the buggane, and the warning of the glashtin. Gorry feared the conquest, plundering and destruction of his land by these hoarding gluttons who were stealing life away from others. He could still smell the foul odor nearby and hear the flies buzzing. This time, however, in a state of consciousness between hallucination and reality, as he looked around, he believed he saw the lifeless body of an unclothed woman lying in the field. He recognized her as one of the fair people. She was Mona, whom he adored above all others. A stone-tipped arrow had pierced her chest. The distinguishable carving was well-known to Gorry. His mind filled with rage as he watched the grass in the fields melt away toward the sea, leaving only barren rock. The trees in the forest scorched and burned and withered away into ashes. The streams and wells dried, and the creatures of the land perished.

Upon supposing this destruction, a raven appeared to him and spoke saying, "The light one came with his frivolous foot soldiers and mocked nature, attacking her weakness, her vulnerability, her innocence. Because of his thoughtlessness, the Spirit of Man has marked him with a crown of gray. He and his men now drunkenly slumber, celebrating their cowardly victory. The laws have been violated." The raven continued, "Nature has become unbalanced. Without secure foundation, the structure will surely fall. The sacrificial lambs have been killed and eaten ahead of the summer grazing. Evil has been unleashed and the shepherds mourn. The seasons have been disturbed and the people will starve: they will turn on each other."

Alone and distraught, Gorry tried to reason this was just a dream. Yet he had seen through these visions, the weight of it all was on his shoulders.

The raven cried again, "It is said, 'He who steals the eggs of the wren will have their own house struck by fire!'" Then the raven looked at Gorry and said, "Someone must avenge the innocent. They seek to destroy Mona. Will no one, not even you the gardener, defend her?"

In the dark of night, Gorry sprung up from his bed of leaves. The night air had cooled and there was a mist over the entire field where he and the dog slept. This was a welcomed sign, he thought, a reminder Mannan was present on the Island, protecting her from enemies. However, he understood a different adversary, a foe already on shore, was attacking creation. All the creatures were threatened. He felt his heart pounding through his chest and great pressure inside his head. Surely, all could see this onslaught of clandestine insult to the kingdom, he reasoned. Yet no one showed outrage. No dire curses vowing to destroy the clear enemy could be heard.

Fury consumed his thoughts, until finally he cried out. "God of creation! God of man, where are you? You must be sleeping! Are your eyes closed, your ears deaf, so you do not see nor hear? Have you left all you created alone to fend for itself? Did you make all of this, the glen, the garden, this whole earth, and her inhabitants, then walk away? Does the sun rise only for the purpose of setting? Does man awaken, only to return to sleeping? Are we given life, only to die? All you have made, everything pure and perfect, is crumbling! Where are you, right now, this very minute? I cry out to you, and you do not respond! Are you there or have you abandoned me?"

Gorry stood, cold and shivering in the stark stillness. "I am alone," he said, looking out around and across the field. "I can hear and speak to the living and the spirit world, but I am now completely alone. Why? Why did you leave me? When I was a child, I had great respect for you, yet you showed me little compassion. You abandoned me, leaving me to protect myself. I wander the garden each day, accepting responsibility to oversee it. I became the father of the garden. Am I not also then father of all the land? By my blood, by those before me, does it not stand to reason I should be king? The King of Man? Since you have abandoned us and are not here to set the world back on course I will fulfill the role of sovereign royal! I will protect my land and my creatures! Even though you were not there when I needed you as a child, I still believed. Now, I believe no longer!"

As he spoke, his whole countenance began to change. His voice became a snarl like that of a rabid animal. Patches of thick, bristly hair sprouted out over all his flesh. The silky locks of black hair on his head became coarse and wiry and his eyes glowed like torches. Gorry looked to the sky, his eyes weeping, his face distorted with great sorrow, and his arms stretched out at his sides.

He growled as he spoke with great agony, saying, "Why don't you save your creation from this plight? These men? Instead, you make them masters, letting them destroy it, abolishing your creation, insulting your presence."

He pointed to the field, then to the heavens, in a sweeping motion. "If you, who stand above all others, are the god of these men . . . then you are not my god!"

When he spoke these words, the sky rumbled and the ground quaked under his feet. Consumed only with taking revenge on his proclaimed enemy, those who would destroy his land, Gorry savagely tore the clothing from his body, emulating the Gaesatae warriors. He had declared his own war!

The angry sky roared again as Gorry cried out, this time with a great sorrowful moan. When he did this, the whole Island and all its inhabitants heard. No one had ever witnessed lamentation of an unrestrained soul tormented with such anguish, and all were afraid. Gorry growled wildly as his spirit left him and his body reshaped into that of a fierce buggane.

Hurtling over the ground as a soldier on a mission of doom, devoid of all reason, Gorry headed back toward the village. Oblivious now to human pain, he ran from the farmer's field back to the valley separating him from Holmtown. Along the way, he hacked enough gorse as he supposed he might need to secure victory over his enemy. Some he left burning high upon the hill, above the settlement. Some he carried as bundles on his shoulders. Speaking to each as if a living being, saying, "My garden will be my army, removing the vermin and restoring its splendor. For this, you will always be known for your beauty, as well as your remedies. From this day forward, future generations will marvel at your golden leaves. You die this day for a noble purpose."

As he lit some bound branches to carry as torches, he continued, "This is what I, Gorry, King of Man, must do. I will cure the disease ravaging my land. I will end this plague brought upon Man by the callous aggression of men." He looked at the valley below, saying, "I bless the curlew, the goat and the cock! Moreover, I command you, Manannan, back away this hour. You with your great warriors, flee from my presence at once. For I am now the patron saint."

Then from atop the hill, he let go and ran into the valley to the sleeping settlement of tiny homes lining the shore beside the campsites. He entered the settlement from the south, along the eastern fields, searching until he found the main road traveled by visitors and merchants. As he ran through the narrow street he began to set fire to the thatched rooftops of several of the homes: the first of which was Fin's. As his flaming torch touched the dry straw roofs, they immediately burst into flames. Behind him, cries of the people awakened by the smoke rang through the air. He reasoned as he ran, I am not like them. They don't know me, or what harm they do. They are complacent, like the farmer's animal, well attended, yet unaware of the butcher's knife which is sure to come.

Hurrying to escape the village, the same way as he had entered, Gorry saw a shadowy figure on the road ahead. A small boy had stumbled out into the street holding his arms outstretched. Gorry was running so fast he could not avoid him, knocking him to the ground.

When he did this, Gorry immediately stopped to check on the little boy, asking in a less fearsome tone, "Are you hurt?" The little boy looked familiar to Gorry. He asked, "Who are you? Do I know you?"

The little boy said, "I am lost in this darkness and cannot see. Evil has been brought upon my home and I do not understand it. I am alone." He stood, again raising his arms, and reaching out.

Gorry now recognized the little, orphaned, blind boy he had rescued from the harness. "I know you. We have met. Stay where you are child," he commanded, his voice becoming more normal again. "Wait here for your grandmother. Be patient and know your god is near. He will protect you. I am sorry you have suffered this evil."

Devastated by the reality of what he had done, Gorry let out a great sigh, then turned and ran from the settlement without lighting any more fires.

As he climbed the hill toward the Saints' well, the sky behind him filled with billowing clouds, roaring thunder, and bright flashes of lightning. A torrential rain came pouring from the sky, right over the settlement. The fires Gorry set were almost instantly extinguished, barely burning any of the rooftops. Gorry could see the people scurrying about in the settlement, trying to make sense of what had occurred. Watching the commotion, he remembered the little boy and what he had said. Gorry wept with great sorrow and fell to the ground, thinking of what he had done. His eyes grew dim, the hair on his body fell off, making small piles on the ground, then turning to ash. He felt the pain of his limbs twisting, shifting back into their normal position. Showers steadily drenched the earth around him as he crouched, naked and alone.

"Great Spirit," I have been a fool. I lost all reason, believing myself both god and man. I have been poisoned by my own vanity."

The settlement became smaller and more obscure with each step further along the spine of the hill he walked. It completely faded from his sight as he reached the highest peak and walked into the clouds along the cliffs. Beyond the cliffs was his home, his glen with the stream gracefully flowing to the sea. Gorry continued on through the darkness, along the slope of the hill. Nearby, he could see a raised embankment surrounding the remains of a sacred mound made of rocks and covered in a shell of earth. An entrance to a small chamber with walls of white stone was barely visible along the edge of the mound. There, in this holy place, Gorry found refuge from the storm, so, he rested a while.

The rhythm of the rain lulled him, causing him to fall into a deep sleep. His great act of revenge faded from his thoughts, replaced by a familiar, recurring nightmare.

Brilliant intermittent flashes of light illuminated blackened skies, while earth-shaking explosions of thunder rumbled continuously amidst torrential rain. Howling gusts of wind cried in ghostly chorus, as if God's full fury and rage was damning every living thing in its path. The sea heaved, with dark waves rising and crashing onto jagged rocks and boulders lining the shore. From a distance, a young Gorry could see hollow-faced figures floating along the edge of the nearby cliff: lost spirits with no eyes or noses, whose mouths were nothing but dark ovals. They were without clothing, their bodies lacking any identity, instead appearing covered only by bluish-gray rotting skin, dripping from their bones. As he continued to watch this hellish scene unfold he knew he had been here before. Gorry saw his father and heard his raging voice; his mother cowering on the ground. All the flashes and rumbles of thunder continued. All the haunting spirits invaded his mind as each time before. The whole scene played out just the same, once again, until the end. This time the end was different. Gorry saw his father at the edge of the cliff. Confusion consumed him as his father turned his back to the sea and shouted.

"Will no one watch with me this hour? Is my life only to be imagined?" he cried, looking past Gorry.

"I am here with you, father!"

His father continued to speak as if he had not heard him. "I have been betrayed. My vanity has distorted my reason. Care not of my passing."

"Father, I am here with you!"

"Mona." His father wept, still gazing beyond. "My beautiful lily of the pond."

Everything in the nightmare was same, except this time when his father lowered his gaze, looking directly into Gorry's eyes, he uttered the words, "Forgive me not, boy, for this path I choose." Then his father turned and leapt from the cliff, fading into the dark abyss.

Fin and the Fianna Return

A legend was he and his mighty men
The tales of Fin do convey
Handsome and wise, his manner was curt
His name lives on at end of day

Dew lay like syrup on the leaves and fallen branches scattered across the field by the previous night's storm. Some of the hunting party were already huddled around the crackling embers of the campfire, trying to fend off the crispness of the morning, when Fin roused. Most had already begun to fill themselves on dark bread and wine they had not finished the night before, complaining to each other about the heavy rain, thunder and lightning disturbing their sleep. Hearing their grumbling, Fin left his tent and joined them by the fire.

"What should we think of the cry of the buggane?" one man asked. "The one who lamented so loudly before the storm? Such a miserable wailing sound I've never heard."

On they went with stories of strange sounds and ghostly movements through the tall grasses they each had witnessed. Finally, when all the men were awake, and had set their bags, the call was made to leave the farmer's fields and head home. Fin sent his son, Oshin, and another one of his men to pay the farmer for the lambs and explain the state of affairs.

It was barely midmorning as the hunting party approached the settlement. Evidence of the storm grew worse the closer they came. Much debris was strewn across the land in every direction. Women and children were busy clearing branches from the streets and trying to make order of things again. When the men arrived at the edge of the village, an old woman walked up to the group. She spoke staring directly at Fin, with her finger raised, pointing in a circular motion at all of his men.

"He who disturbs the wren or her offspring will find his house destroyed by fire. Who among you disturbed the wren and angered the buggane?"

"What foolishness is this?" he asked his men.

"She speaks of an ancient curse," one replied.

"Go away old woman. Leave us alone. I do not heed your ancient mysticism."

As he and his men traveled further into the village they were approached by Father Druce and Aine, who asked them to come to the house of the Minister of Justice to discuss a serious matter. Other guildsmen, who had not gone on the hunt with Fin, were already assembled.

"What is this matter for discussion?" Fin asked entering the Minister's home with Aine and Father Druce.

"Just before the storm, in the dark of night, a buggane ran through the streets and attempted to burn several of our homes with a torch. We were fortunate though. The rains came soon after so only some rooftops were damaged. Yours was the most scarred Fin," replied the Minister.

Fin was surprised. "What causes you to think it was the work of a buggane?" he asked.

"We heard the cry in the night. Not long after, our

roofs were on fire. Then the storm raged," explained one of the Guildsmen.

"What's more, this morning we heard the old woman, Leece's mother, wandering the streets talking about an ancient curse," said Aine.

"Bring the old woman to this place," the Minister of Justice commanded one of his young assistants. "Perhaps she can explain further."

A few moments later, the assistant returned with the old woman, who stood trembling in great fear. Beside her was the little blind boy.

"Old woman," commanded the Minister, "tell us of the ancient curse you have been speaking in the village."

The old woman hesitated, fearing she and the child would face the sharp edge of a sword if she spoke. Slowly, timidly, she gazed around the room and repeated the curse. "If a man disturbs the wren's nest, his home will be destroyed by fire."

"Ha! Who here, in the settlement, still believes this old fable?" Fin asked mockingly.

The people around him turned to one another, mumbling indistinctive chatter, but no one answered.

"Woman," the Minister ordered, "tell what you know of this evil that has been done."

"The actions of the creature that set fire to the rooftops was done to avenge nature," she began cautiously. "He is not from within the settlement. The wren gave a warning to this man who can hear and speak both to the living and spirit world. He lives alone, beyond the woods in the glen south of here. He is one who lives among the fair people and protects all of creation."

When she said this, those gathered knew she spoke of Gorry and they were greatly dismayed.

"How do you know of this, old woman?" Fin asked.

"I heard the anguished howl of the buggane in the night. Then, the wren appeared to me during the storm and told me all I have now told you. The boy here met the creature on the road as he was fleeing the village."

"Iniuria," said Farther Druce, "do you know the man you speak of?"

"I only know what the wren told me. I did not see the man myself." She grabbed the shoulders of the small child and pulled him before her facing the Minister. "My grandson saw him. Didn't you boy?"

"Iniuria, you speak of Gorry, your oldest son," Father Druce told her.

"What? . . . No! It cannot be true. My Gorry was lost to me years ago in a great storm. I never saw him again after that night. He perished with his father."

"No, Iniuria, young Gorry made his way to the village a few days later. He told us of the storm. We gave him shelter at the orphanage. He stayed a few years before running away to live back in the glen."

No . . . it cannot be true," she said as she began to weep. Holding the little boy close, she murmured softly, "What have I done? My sins have greatly overshadowed me."

"What shall we do?" the Minister asked, turning his attention to Fin. "How do you suggest we resolve this? Your home was the most damaged. What punishment is compensatory for harm done to the property of a guildsman by this vassal?"

Fin became keenly aware of his place in this situation. He knew to be careful answering the Minister's question. The laws of ancient time had begun to fade to a new system of justice. Rights and privileges once given only to the upper classes were now to be given also to the commoner. The new laws required all men, regardless of class or status, be judged by equal measure for crimes committed. Fin knew he too could be held accountable for his actions, if they were known. As he considered the curse from the old woman, he cunningly devised a response to the Minister. "Bring the child here woman," he directed. "You say the blind boy saw him? Then we will ask him to bear witness in order to decide."

The young boy cowered next to his grandmother.

Aine, seeing his fear, stepped forward and said, "You and your men scare the child with all this, Fin. Let me take him and speak to him alone where he does not fear your stature and your swords."

The Minister, Fin and the old woman agreed, so Aine took the boy away into another room. Once they were alone, Aine and the child sat quietly for a moment while she gently held his hands. Then in a tender voice she said.

"Do not be frightened, child. Speak clearly, tell me the truth of what happened?"

"Well . . . I woke from sleep when the thunder clashed and the rain began to fall. I called out for my grandmother, but she did not come, so I was afraid."

"Yes, go on."

"I could smell the smoke of the fires and feared for my

life. I ran out into the street and bumped into a man there. He was very kind, stopping to see if I was okay."

"What more?"

"I said I could not see. The man told me to stay there and wait until my grandmother could find me. He said not to worry, for God was near and would protect me. He told me he was sorry for the evil. His voice was strange, but I remember him. He was the man that saved me from choking when I caught myself on a horse harness the night of the dance."

"What happened next?"

"Well, I heard him let out a sorrowful sigh and then he ran away."

Aine paused for a moment, thinking about his words. They sparked a memory in her of another little boy. A misunderstood young lad who lived with her uncle at the orphanage. A boy whom she had often seen standing alone, apart from the other children: young Gorry.

A sudden knocking startled her. She held her finger over the boy's lips. When Aine answered the door, the man named Kaughin who had spoken to Gorry at his campsite the morning of the battle was there.

"My apologies, miss. I pray I haven't arrived too late. I have a message for you," he spoke with labored breath, as he had hurried through the village to find her. "Aine, I understand you do not know me, nonetheless the gods have guided me to you this day. I have come here by their urging. I must speak with you."

"Please come in."

Kaughin entered the room. He looked at the boy, then

at Aine. "I feel the spirits have brought the three of us together for a purpose."

"Please sir, what is the message? What is so important?" asked Aine.

"I hope what I tell you now might somehow be helpful. You see, I spoke with a man during the wake, a man whom I have known since our youth. When in conversation, he reminded me of a young girl whom he had admired, loved since they were both young."

"Yes, go on."

"One day, when we, he and I, were running about the settlement, we stumbled upon the home of the girl's uncle, whom she visited during the summer months. I hid behind some hedges, while he gathered his courage and set upon her stoop a lovely yellow flower. When he heard the door handle turn, he hurried to me in hiding, and we ran fast away. This man told me the other day, he would like to pay the girl, now a young woman, some attention, but he could not bring himself to approach her. He said he was waiting for her to remember. He told me she would know him by the yellow flower he left on her doorstep."

Aine instantly remembered one morning, finding a yellow flower placed neatly on her uncle's front stoop. She had opened the door just in time to see some boys running away, but could not make out who they were.

"Go on, sir. Why could he not approach her?"

"Because he was of a lower station. He felt she would turn him away. He ran away fast so as not to be seen."

"Lower station? I don't understand. Who do you speak of, sir?"

"Miss, it was young Gorry. And you are the young woman he admires."

A stunned Aine thanked Kaughin as he left the room.

She had always favored Gorry over other boys, even dreamt of them together, but her family had strictly encouraged her otherwise, saying he was not of their class. She lived among those who judged others beneath their station, believing the less fortunate were deserving of their fate. She remembered Gorry was always so genuine, so kind, but also so sad and alone. Thoughts of the past several days, scenes from the wake, the funeral, her dreams, danced back and forth in her head. She remembered finding Gorry's poem to Mona, reading of his devotion and kindness. She recalled learning her jealousy was unfounded. His commitment was to his land, not another woman. She remembered dreaming she would one day reveal to him her true love and they would go away together to the meadow of soft, green grass. The little boy stirred in his seat, bringing Aine's thoughts back to the situation at hand.

Aine sighed deeply as she realized the gravity of her position this day. Her explanation to the Minister and guildsmen, of what the little boy confided in her, would determine their judgement for the iniquities Gorry had committed. Then, she recollected the words of Father Druce, when he explained to her Rahab acted with a pure heart, true to her understanding of God and of the Holy Scriptures.

Aine looked into the face of the small innocent boy in front of her. *He sees with a pure heart, not with judgemental eyes,* she thought. Aine addressed the boy.

"So, you say the man that set the fires told you God was near and would protect you? That he was sorry for the evil?"

"Yes," said the child as he began to cry. "He was good and kind to me."

"Do not cry, little one, do not be afraid. You have given me great sight. I understand what we must do."

When Aine and the little boy returned to the outer room, the people waiting became excited and wanted to know what was said. Aine knew the power she held in that moment. She knew her words could condemn a man, a man she truly believed to be decent and gentle, possibly to death. Or, she hoped, maybe they will understand and forgive. So Aine said this:

"Those of certain rights and privileges have summoned the voice of the overlooked, the poor, to participate in this decision of justice. This innocent child has been called upon as witness for an alleged crime: Forced to act as if condoning the laws of this community which, for years past, prohibited his family, his ancestors, from attaining the same rights and privileges. This boy sees with a pure heart, not judgemental eyes. He explained to me all he witnessed, and speaks favorably of the accused. Have no fear child. Share with them what you have just told me."

The boy stood beside Aine holding her hand. He spoke into the air looking at no one, but to everyone he said. "I believe the man that burned the rooftops had no evil in his heart. He showed me compassion even in the midst of his own suffering."

Now the boy sensed something odd, so he turned and, possibly by accident, gazed directly at Fin, saying, "When a person is hurt, becomes weakened and wounded by someone else's bad deed, they might turn to do evil and sin. Not as revenge, but rather as an attempt to right a wrong, protect the innocent. I feel the man that did this was hurting and conflicted in his mind and soul."

The guildsmen and Minister of Justice were impressed with the words the boy spoke, for he was very young and they did not expect such wisdom to come from him.

Fin, uneasy about the boy's compelling gaze, inquired, "What is this you speak of?"

The boy hesitated and, before he could answer, Fin and Oshin's daughters stepped forward from the crowd.

"Turn your sightless gaze upon me boy. I must speak," Fin's daughter said calmly. "It was us, Father, together with our friends," she said looking at Fin. "We burned Gorry's feet as he slept."

"We wished to embarrass him for not accepting your invitation to the hunt," confessed Oshin's daughter. "Now I see we have been heartless in our actions."

When she said this, the elders were aghast. "We blamed Gorry alone for this crime, however, we see now, these girls, with their careless act, provoked him."

"Your thoughtless actions incited his anger," said Father Druce. "You are as much to blame for the suffering of the village as Gorry. We must all remember people act as they are treated."

"He is right," said Fin, stepping forward. "I must share

the blame in part. My men and I scoffed at Gorry for not joining us in the hunt. We broke the law of nature and killed the new lambs out of season. I am the one who disturbed the wren's nest. If anyone deserves punishment, it is me. I see the foolishness of my ways and beg your forgiveness." Touching his daughter on the shoulder, Fin said to her, "Thank you for your honesty my child. That was very brave. You have taught me much."

Aine addressed the Minister of Justice. "Sir, a great wrong has been done by many, but all can be righted through understanding and compassion. If we are to survive and progress as a society, I say we need to learn to accept and embrace those with different ideologies and beliefs. We need to show forgiveness, rather than vengeance."

Those gathered nodded in agreement and declared they would march along the shore until they found Gorry to tell him all was forgiven. They would let him know that he would always be welcome.

The Minister of Justice proclaimed. "From this day forward, we will seek to understand that which is new to us and those with different views. Everyone's voice shall be heard equally."

Then Aine whispered in the little boy's ear. "Today, you have not only saved a man's life, you have given vision to a village blinded by the ways of man."

The Last Judgement

Sorrow consumes the thoughts of man
Whose drive preempts sound thought
His goal may be clear, his intentions pure
As the Garden of Gethsemane taught

The sun, high overhead, had already dissipated the morning fog and warmed the ground when Gorry finally awoke. Crawling out of the sacred chamber, exhausted from madness, and dreaming, his body still covered only with mud, he made his way on hands and knees along the hill to the edge of the cliff. His head ached with such throbbing it was hard to focus. Gorry mournfully recalled his deeds, thinking of how the people of the settlement might take revenge.

A few feet away, a flock of gulls rose in flight, bursting from their perch along the cliff, fluttering skyward. "Fides?" he cried out, standing up as close to the cliff's edge as he could, looking far out across the rippling gray water. "Father, is that you?" Then he turned around, away from the sea, to gaze at the land.

"No," he spoke with great sorrow. "I have no father, no mother, no spirit to guide me. All have taken leave of me. My flesh was weak and I succumbed to the torment of others. I committed a great sin for which no one is to blame except myself. The choice I made to seek revenge caused much pain and suffering to the innocent. I am ashamed."

He looked south, to the glen, pleading, "Will no one watch with me this hour? Is my future only to be imagined?" He looked north, at the settlement laying peacefully beyond the hill. "Am I so like my father that self-importance distorted my reason, and brought me to this demise?"

Gazing over the land, Gorry saw the approaching crowd marching toward him, clanging tools and calling out. Given the distance, and the roar of the ocean, Gorry could not hear clearly their words. Surely they had come to punish him for his deeds, he thought. Remorse and utter hopelessness filled his being.

"Take your rest, good people of Holmtown. Care not of my passing. Forgive me," he shouted toward the approaching villagers. "Great God Odin, I beseech you, come hither and guide my undeserving soul to Valhalla."

Gorry could now only hear the undulating waves battering the rocky shoreline below. "My time has come. The winds are strong at my back and the sun is warm on my face."

He watched the crowd drawing nearer and thought he caught a glimpse of Aine. In a more wistful tone, as if she were standing beside him, Gorry continued, "Aine, you are the lovely yellow flower in the garden."

Then he looked across the fields as far as he could see. "Mona, you are the beautiful lily of the pond."

It was there and then, in that moment on the edge of the cliff, while Gorry faced the land in all its glory, envisioning Mona, the beautiful lily, and Aine, the lovely yellow flower, he realized it was his decision which way his path would wind next. He was free to make the most important choice he had ever made. And so, he did.

THE END

Chapter Three

Shifting sideways in the chair stirs me awake, I must have passed out. Blinking a few times, I try to focus. The soft glow of the small reading lamp illuminates only the immediate area around the table and chair. Dim shadows fill the space beyond. As the second hand of the clock echoes in the quiet of the morning, I sluggishly remember where I am and how I spent my night. I did as Elan suggested. I read the book, the entire book, cover to cover. It was an uncomfortable emotional rollercoaster, but, I gained a new understanding, a greater appreciation, of how an ancient and diverse society coexisted during times of profound change.

Picking up the book from the floor, a thought crosses my mind. I reach for the binder containing Lottie's draft ideas and remove the contents. Gingerly untying the manuscript, I transfer the yellowed parchment pages into the binder, then tie the pages from the notebook together between the old manuscript cover and place it on the table. I put the binder, now holding the original manuscript, into a secret bottom pocket of my overnight bag. *That should keep it safe*, I think.

I fumble through my satchel, grab my journal, retrieve a pen from another pocket, and begin to write.

Thursday, March 16, 2000
Sweetie,
It has been just a day since I last wrote, yet it seems like

forever. I find there is scarcely a moment I don't think of us. I miss your soft voice, your eyes, and the tender touch of your hands. Forgive me, I know I write this every day, but that's because it is true every day. There is no other like you. Yesterday, a man called what we have a pairing of souls. I think he was right. We have spent a lifetime together living an adventure unlike anyone else. You are so much of me, of who I am. Since the tragic news, my heart has become increasingly hollow. Each day I am barely able to manage civility toward others. Inside I rage with grief. I question my thoughts, my actions, my sanity. Every move I make, or word I speak, feels automated and empty. I have always been nothing more than a reflection of you, of your grace and wisdom and now the mirror is foggy. I thought of you last night as I read. Your character, your spirit, was alive in the book you left for me. The story was so real I thought I caught a glimpse of you. Who were you? Which character? Were you the young woman Aine. Were you Mona? Both? You see, I love you in so many ways. Through you, my happiness was always so easily accessible. Now, I longingly search for what has become inaccessible. My soul yearns for you. I love you Lottie. I always have and I always will.

Lowering the pen, I place it exactly perpendicular to the journal. I rise slowly and go to the window where, beyond the promenade, lies the vast, eternal sea giving a sense of abundance of life.

I love you. I always have and I always will. This was our phrase, spoken with gentle wittiness, yet also with such earnestness. *'I love you John,'* she would say. *'I love you Lottie,'* I would respond, looking deep into her eyes. She would giggle sweetly, anticipating the continuation. *'I always have . . . and I always will.'* She would sigh and give me a quick hug and kiss. Trying to add to the rhyme was a game we played without end. We were never able to find just the right words. We wanted the perfect ending. As the years slipped by, fading into the past, we never felt any urgency to complete it.

One day, not so long ago, after trying many times to add a new line, we paused in our playfulness. It was the end of a long day and our tongues were tired of the endless banter of two lovers in love, always sharing thoughts and planning our next adventure. We spoke of the reality of mortality, the frailty of human life, the inevitability of death. We timidly and reluctantly moved through a very serious discussion of what we would do if given the opportunity to decide. She spoke of the length and expense of any extended end of life treatment. She said she did not want to become a burden to me or our children. I told her I hated the thought of a nursing home or hospital draining our savings just to keep me alive. Besides, she would need as much as possible after my death for living expenses. We both agreed we should not prolong any suffering. Not just for us, but for all those who loved us.

These conversations only occasionally arose on rainy days while the two of us sat facing each other, drinks in hand, pretending to be heroes, proclaiming a decision for an exit based on our hypothetical scenarios. Oh, how bold and unassuming we were. How strongly we spoke. How bravely we boasted as if absent of fear. Man is always full of wisdom and strength, until he is forced to face the front lines of a battle. A short year later, when we learned the results of her medical tests, it all became bitterly real. The battle had come to us. Oh, dear God, forgive me, my love, if I somehow persuaded your thoughts in some way. God forgive us both if we convinced ourselves to act hastily, foolishly, hastening a premature end.

Standing there, I study each wave as it splashes onto the shoreline and then humbly rolls back out into the abyss, surrendering itself again to the sea. The gentle lapping of waves is calming, reassuring, and soothes the madness plaguing my soul. The sky, still gray, has become a lighter shade, ushering in another day, giving way to yet one more weary night.

I shuffle to the bathroom. My arthritic fingers struggle to open the small travel bag. After generously applying shaving gel to help the razor glide gently over this uneven terrain, I methodically move the razor across my face: first left, then right, then down. As I step into the shower, steam fills the small room like a dense fog. I cannot help but dream of her again. Every morning of this journey is the same. Always the same dream, always the same ending, always the same disappointment and emptiness.

With the usual preparations for the day complete and double checked, I grab my coat and room key to seek out some freshly brewed coffee, the scent of which is wafting through the air, beckoning me. There is a rap at the door just as I reach for the handle. Peering through the small hole I recognize it is Mercher.

"Good morning, Mister Mercher," I greet him as I open the door.

"Good morning, Mister Christian. I hope I am not too early. I read the sign on the way out last night and it said breakfast was served starting at six, Monday through Saturday. And, well it being Thursday, I assumed you would already be awake encouraged by the aroma of fresh coffee."

"Yes, it's fine. I've been up a while already."

Mercher, wearing a tan sport jacket, blue shirt and faded dungarees, loosely slouched around the tops of well-worn boots, enters the room. He at once notices what appears to be the manuscript on the table beside the chair. "Did you get a chance to start the book?" he asks.

"Why yes I did. I read it all the way through."

"The whole book? You read the whole thing last night?"

"Yes, actually. It took much of the night. I passed out in the chair. I have to say I am exhausted."

"Fascinating."

"Yes, it was very fascinating, really."

"I always find these ancient stories quite entertaining, Christian, although, probably a bit more romanticized than historically correct."

"Well as far as this story is concerned, all I could think about as I read, was what it might have meant to my wife. How did she interpret the story?"

"You know, Christian, I have never mentioned it to anyone, but your Lottie reminded me quite a bit of my dear wife, Jean. She died several years ago, but oh, what a lively spirit she had while she was alive. I sensed that same vibrant essence in Lottie."

"That's just it, I feel as though her life force was navigating within the text, a part of her trying to tell me something."

"Well, if it spoke to you that deeply, if the prose was true, and the characters clearly defined through your imagining, then it must have been well-written indeed. I look forward to reviewing it. I do wonder when the original is to arrive in my department. I will have to ask Elan," he says looking curiously at the book.

"Are you in a hurry, Mercher? Do we need to get going?"

"Oh no, not at all my good man, no hurry."

"Great, would you like to join me downstairs for coffee and a bite to eat?"

"Certainly, that is why I came early, my good man."

Breakfast is served in the lounge on the first floor. The morning hostess is the same middle-aged woman I saw peering out of the kitchen window yesterday, the older version of the pregnant young girl from the photograph. This morning she is wearing a blue, flowery dress and white apron folded at her waist.

Greeting us with a warm smile she says, "Morning gents, sit anywhere. Help yourself to the breakfast bar. I just made a fresh pot of coffee. If there is anything else I can get you fellows, just let me know. I'm Mary. You met my daughter Maggie yesterday. She owns the place . . . calls me her business partner. Really, all I do is help out where I can."

As Mary attends to other guests, we pour our coffee and choose from an assortment of pastries, breads and fruit.

Seating ourselves at a small table in the corner near the dart board, Mercher pulls a map from his vest pocket. He opens it, and points.

"You see we have a short trip. It is only about a ten-minute drive to Saint John's. We will be stopping there to meet Elan and Vikki before we get to the dig site. It is beautiful countryside with a lot of history."

"Mercher, I want you to know how much I appreciate your escorting me to collect Lottie's things. It has been a difficult time. It is so kind of you to assist me with this."

"Do not mention it my good man, happy to help."

We finish our pastries and coffee just as Mary comes over to our table.

"Can I get you anything else, gents? Something to take away?"

"I think I'm good, how about you, Mercher?"

"Oh, thank you, no. I am fine. I do think I will fetch us a brolly or two from the lobby. This mist is just irritating enough to make you think you need one."

Peel Road winds out of town, gently rising past rural golf courses, a sports center, and surrounding neighborhoods. We pass roads with names like 'New Castletown' and 'Quarter Bridge.' The road runs parallel to the River Dhoo to its headwaters and source near a plantation in the center of the isle. We pass the new Parish Church of Marown. The old parish lies across the river, hidden in the hills to the south. Mercher tells me Saint

Patrick's Chair sits nearby and the remains of the Druidical Stone Circles of Glen Darragh are also in this area. On the road, a little beyond Crosby, in a field on the northern side, is the Church of Saint Trinian, roofless and in a ruinous state. The field is elevated. A small stone wall separates it from the road. My guide boasts of its lonely, albeit peaceful state. The nave and chancel are without architectural division, built of clay flagstone from local mines, he tells me. The legend is, it never had a roof thanks to the fabled buggane.

A short distance further, we cross Curragh Road arriving at Saint John's, a sleepy little village in the center of the isle. It is the home of Tynwald Hill, the original assembly place for the Island's parliament. The village is nestled peacefully in a central valley framed by Slieau Whallian, a steep hill to the south and the Tynwald National Park and arboretum situated on the north. Mercher pulls up in front of a quaint inn and grill at the intersection of Peel Road, where Glen Mooar Road goes north and Station Road heads south. Witches Hill looms in the background providing a colorful legend of darker times when those thought to be sorceresses were rolled from the top of the hill in spiked barrels. If they were alive at the bottom, they were judged to be enchantresses and put to death.

"This is where Doctor Clemmings, Vikki, said she would meet us," Mercher says, interrupting my daydreaming. "Shall we go in for another cup of coffee while we wait?"

"Sure, I could do with a bit more."

The turn of the century inn we have stopped at is adorned with several black roof peaks. On opposite ends of the building are large chimneys billowing smoke, swirling skyward, disappearing into the cloud-laden heavens. The interior of the inn is clean and warm. A well-groomed young man, wearing a shiny gray vest over a crisp, white shirt and slim black tie, is behind the bar. Watching him connect small plastic hoses from pressurized tanks of carbonated beverages to the taps, I think how out of place he appears in this rural setting.

"Nice restaurant you have here," I offer.

"Not a restaurant. It's a pub. We also just happen to serve good food," he says with a smirk.

"I stand corrected . . . Right now, I'm interested in your coffee."

"You're in luck mate. We've got the best in town. I'll get one of the girls to bring you gents a cup. Cream and sugar are on the tables. Sit anywhere you like."

Mercher and I find a table near a window on the outside corner facing the road. A large stone fireplace situated in the middle of the wall across from where we sit is roaring, keeping the room warm. Framed snapshots of men and their motorcycles stretch across the long wooden mantle; a large, autographed, framed picture sits prominently in the middle.

"Jeffries," the young man speaks up from behind the bar, pointing to the photograph. "Won again at the TT last year. He came here right after the races and signed that photograph for me. Hope he wins again this year, he's a nice bloke."

A gangly young girl with short-cropped blondish-brown hair, highlighted with a few fluorescent pink stripes, approaches our table. The fingers of her left hand are woven through handles of two coffee mugs with the inn logo embossed in green on one side. Her right hand firmly grasps a steaming pot of freshly brewed coffee.

"Morning," she says in a crackly voice, while chomping heartily on a piece of chewing gum. Her bright-green eyes are surrounded by a sea of freckles. "Can I get you a menu or anything?" she asks filling both cups to the brim.

Mercher frowns, shaking his head from side to side.

"Nope. I think we're good with just coffee, thanks." I barely get past *'nope'* as she impatiently walks away.

"Would you like cream?" I ask Mercher, as I finish pouring some into my cup.

"Oh no, thank you. I take mine black."

A squeaky, repetitive, pop tune can be heard coming from a small transistor radio behind the bar. A young man stocking the shelves with freshly washed glasses is swaying to the beat and mouthing some of the incoherent lyrics. Our eyes meet, and, seemingly embarrassed, he quickly reaches over to adjust the volume. I peer out the window in time to see a safari-like, dark pea-green vehicle, with sandstone colored accents and splashes of dried mud around the wheel wells, speedily enter the parking area. It stops so abruptly, the two occupants lurch forward in their seats. Both hurriedly unhook their seatbelts and fling open their doors.

Mercher spots the distinguishable university logo on

the passenger door. "Solis a terra: From the Ground to the Sun," he reads aloud.

These profound words remind me of high school trigonometry. Solving the unknown side of a triangle; figuring out the distance from the ground to the sun. The puzzle is solved only if, and when, you know the length of the other two sides. *But, even if you do not know the length of the other two, the distance is still the same*, I think.

Vikki and Elan stumble through the front door and hastily walk toward our table. The green-eyed girl, still chewing vigorously on her gum, returns.

"Can I get you two coffee or tea, or anything?" she inquires.

Vikki adjusts her glasses looking sternly at the girl who has no idea her incessant chomping is both unprofessional and unsophisticated.

"I think we are ready to leave," I say. "Will a couple of dollars cover it?"

She looks at me innocently, ignorant of my words. "I don't know the . . . the . . . "

"Conversion. I will pay for it," Mercher says handing her a few pounds.

"Let's all go together in our vehicle," Vikki offers.

Mercher and I look at each other.

"Oh, I don't want to be a bother." I say, recalling the manner in which they arrived.

"Oh, no bother. Besides, there's nowhere to park such a nice car as Mister Mercher's at the site. Once you get off the main road it's too rough to drive anything without high suspension and four-wheel drive."

From the inn, we drive north on a narrow road called Glen Mooar. The road winds past Tynwald Hill, a manmade mound about three meters high with four circular platforms, which are of successively decreasing size, creating a conical shape. The Parish Church of Saint John the Baptist with its tall, narrow spire pointing like a symbol of hope is at the other end of a long grassy concourse. Our path leads us past Glen Mooar snaking through wooded areas with openings into a small pasture. The road narrows as we navigate the hill ahead. To our left, is a steep drop-off into a peaceful glen where the River Neb winds its way from Lambfell Moar through the countryside, eventually emptying into the sea at Peel.

Ahead, I see an old stone house built into the hillside that has fallen into decay and disrepair. A dirt driveway wraps around the front of the long-abandoned dwelling dividing it from overgrown shrubs and vegetation. Elan steers the vehicle slowly onto the drive. Passing the rubble of the once sturdy home, I wonder about the earlier occupants. What was their life like here in this quiet countryside? The rutted terrain jostles our transport as Elan accelerates to advance over a small rise, and then decelerates abruptly stopping at a campsite strewn about with brown canvas tents, small lean-tos, and a variety of shovels and field equipment.

A weather-worn man and a woman with equally sun-dried skin are standing outside one of the tents beside a metal table covered with maps, field books, and two-way radios.

"Mates," Vikki addresses them, extending a gesture as

we approach. "This is Mister Christian, Lottie's husband."

The man, wearing brown dungarees held up by suspenders, his gray hair tied in one long braid down his back, frowns solemnly extending his hand in greeting. "Good woman she was, Lottie."

"Really knew her stuff," adds the woman. "Nice to meet you, Mister Christian."

"It's a pleasure to meet both of you," I reply, feeling uncomfortably out of place once again.

After a few moments of meaningless chitchat, Vikki grabs my elbow and leads me to the other side of the tent with Elan in tow.

"We're doing some test pits here so please watch your step," she cautions. "The ground gets quite muddy when it rains. Even the grass gets very slippery in certain spots."

Mercher stays behind with the man and woman while we cautiously walk about twenty paces from the tent.

"Based on our computer animations and geophysical surveys there's a good chance we'll discover something soon, Neolithic pottery perhaps. Did you see the Ballaharra Stones on your way into the village?" Vikki asks.

"I'm sorry, I really wouldn't know unless they were pointed out to me."

"A local archaeologist led the excavation of a massive tomb with large cremation deposits," Elan explains. "The crypt consisted of two chambers carbon-dated from around 2300 BCE and is believed to be from similar Neolithic origins as King Orry's Grave and Cashtal yn Ard. The vault had six large stones set above ground level, although, only four remain."

"Fascinating," I say, without trying to sound patronizing. I am distracted, in awe of the silent beauty of the vista. I sense a certain mysticism in this ancient land. Closing my eyes to absorb the moment, I try to imagine her here. Try to sense a lingering bit of her aura.

"Plenty of historic sites around," Elan offers. "'Giant's Grave' is right over there at Ballig. The Megaloceros Giganteus, was excavated near here too. Imagine finding that!"

Vikki glances at Elan and nods. She pulls me a little further away in the direction of another tent. Elan deliberately lingers behind.

"You know, Mercher really thought very highly of your wife. He loved her work. We all did. Somehow, I think he felt a deeper connection to her. You see . . . from the pictures I've seen of her, Mercher's wife Jean looked very much like Lottie. The resemblance was uncanny really. Did you know he lost his wife in the Summerland fire back in 1973?"

"No, he mentioned she died, but not how. That is very tragic."

"It's still hard to understand. Fifty-three lives perished and the whole leisure center was destroyed because some juveniles were trying to smoke cigarettes in an abandoned kiosk. Mercher was devastated by her death. The whole thing was so overwhelming he disappeared from society for a while. Even though he was very young when he lost her, he never remarried . . . stayed behind closed doors in his office most of the time. He only recently joined us on this dig. He took on a kind of fatherly role, seemed to be enjoying life again. Something changed in his demeanor when your wife joined us though. He has been very . . . well, melancholy ever since she arrived. He was outwardly kind and complimentary of her work of course. And I know he was happy she was here . . . He never mentioned it, but you could tell it was hard for him. Then, well, something peculiar happened when the manuscript was excavated and he learned it had been given to Lottie to read. His whole demeanor changed from seeming melancholy to very much on edge. He's been acting . . . well . . . just very odd. Keep your guard up, Mister Christian. I think his reaction, his anxiousness, is somehow related to the discovery of the manuscript."

"I understand being melancholy if Lottie reminded him of his wife, but why would he be anxious about her having the manuscript? I don't understand."

"There is something you should know. Mercher is a direct descendant of Bishop Rutter, the man who authored the official written account of the ballad. Some of us think he wants the recently recovered manuscript concealed to protect his family name in case the story ends differently than that of Rutter's."

"A direct descendant . . . very interesting, I didn't realize."

"I agreed with Elan that you should get to read the recovered manuscript in its original state. That's why he delivered it in person. You see, on the Island, legislation requires all items of antiquity to be turned over to the Office of Archives, the department of record. Mercher's official capacity for the past several years has been to lead that department. The woman who gave the manuscript to Lottie felt Mercher might destroy the document or alter it in some way to protect his family. She felt Lottie was trustworthy, a safe third party, who would protect it, preserve it. Lottie understood the law too though. That's why she gave it to Elan and me before she . . . well she was adamant that you get to read it exactly as she had, before Mercher received it. Please promise me you will keep it safe, Mister Christian."

"Yes of course . . . of course I will."

"Where is the manuscript now?"

"Back at the hotel."

"What? Where? Where did you leave it?"

"In my room. It's locked in my room. No one's going to go in there and take it. Don't worry. It will be safe."

Crossing a grassy field, we reach another canvas tent. Upon entering, I recognize, from the pictures she sent me, this is where Lottie worked. Three lawn chairs, a table, a cooler and a storage chest fill the small space. A satchel and a long plastic cylinder lay on the top of the table. Vikki picks up the cylinder and hands it to me.

"Her sketches. The satchel is full of drawing supplies and her other journal. We thought you'd like to have them." Vikki pauses for a moment before she continues. "I hope you don't mind me saying this, but Lottie was quite open about her love for you, Mister Christian. The way she spoke about your relationship, we all knew how much you must love her. She said you always encouraged her to experience as much of life as she could. I am so thankful she was able to come here, to share part of herself with us."

My heart is extremely touched by her kind words. For the first time since receiving the news, I let my guard down and tell her my deepest fear. "I keep thinking, what if there was one more thing I could've done. Something . . . I don't know . . . anything to change the outcome. It feels like it's all a bad dream. Somehow I feel . . . "

"Don't," she interrupts. "Don't ever feel guilty. We all think we can bargain with God, you know, somehow prolong our life. I am certain, from all she told us, you gave her the best life she could have." Saying this, she gently pats my forearm.

In the awkwardness of the moment, I fight to hold back my emotions. Just then, I hear a loud vehicle approaching, saving me from crumbling in anguish in front of this stranger. A moment later an official looking jeep appears from the roadway and pulls into the field. A man, dressed in a police officer's uniform, steps out and approaches Mercher.

Grabbing the satchel from the table, Vikki and I leave the tent and walk hurriedly through the tall grass. Elan joins us on our way to find out what is happening.

"The constable here says he has received word that the ship's captain has requested your presence," Mercher informs me as we approach.

"He and his father are at the hospital," says the constable as he hands Mercher a handwritten note.

"The captain's father has had a turn for the worse, his condition is failing, very dire situation. The note says the old man has requested you come see him, Christian."

"Okay . . . sure. I guess I have collected what I came for.

Do you mind if we go, Mercher?"

Mercher turns to the constable. "Could you give us a lift back to Saint John's, to our car? It is at the inn."

"Yes, of course, sir."

"It was a pleasure to meet you all," I say to the man, woman, Vicki, and Elan.

As I turn, Vikki reaches out and touches my forearm again.

"We miss her," she confides. "She was so kind and genuine . . . as I imagine every daughter wishes her own mother to be."

"Thank you . . . thank you very much," I say as I climb into the back seat of the jeep, cradling the cylinder and satchel to my chest like newborn babies.

The officer is a young man, patient and polite, with short-cropped hair and rugged features. "Have you known him long, sir? Are you related?" he asks.

"No, just met actually. We, um, just seemed to understand one another right off."

The mist turns into a light shower as we retrace our path to town. *We might need those umbrellas after all*, I think, staring emotionlessly out the window. I hear a familiar tune drifting through the vehicle's speakers. Lottie would know this song.

"Who is this?" I ask.

The young constable shrugs.

"Sinatra, my good man," Mercher informs me.

"Sinatra?"

"Yes. Early Sinatra. It is called, 'Paradise'. Very romantic lyrics."

I hear the crooner's smooth baritone voice singing about a woman he loves, holding her hand. How he understands, their thoughts colliding as he looks into her eyes. They kiss and he asks, *'Could I resist?'* I close my eyes for just a moment and imagine she is with me, imagine kissing her.

"What a morning," I whisper with a heavy sigh. "What a journey."

Chapter Four

It is a short distance, but a long drive under these rainy conditions, from the inn at Saint John's to the hospital near Strang, just outside Douglas. The massive medical complex is divided into wings, with signs posted around the building to help guide visitors to their necessary destination. Mercher drops me off at the main entrance.

"Thank you," I say as I step out of the car, still clinging to the cylinder and satchel. "Are you coming in?"

"Not just now, I . . . well . . . I have some pressing business to attend to. It should not take long. I will come back and give you a lift to your hotel when I am finished."

Anticipation, anxiety of what lies ahead, is not unfamiliar to me as I step through the large automated glass doors. Mind-numbing memories of frequent visits with long waiting periods as Lottie moved from test to test, doctor to doctor, assault my being. The unimaginable first opinion haunts me. How reliable was it? How much time did we have? No one could tell us. Everyone had an opinion, especially those who had never been through this. The less of it they knew, the more opinionated they seemed to be. Now, here I am again. I know this situation all too well.

Unaware of how long I have been standing in the entrance, a young woman, dressed in bluish-green hospital scrubs, approaches me. After I explain my situation, she says the old man is most likely in Ward Two, directing me to the west wing of the hospital.

Navigating my way to the ward is like a recurring vision of the many times I walked similar sterile hallways with her, always hoping for a better answer.

"I'm Mister Christian," I announce arriving at the nurse's station. "I'm here to see . . ." *Oh God!* I cut myself off. I have no idea what his name is. I do not even know the name of this old man who thinks so much of me as to ask for me personally in his time of need. All I can tell her is I know his son is Captain Aiza.

The nurse examines her chart. "Mister Ander. Izaro Ander. Doctor Jani is on her way to escort you to his room."

Moments later, a woman wearing a white lab coat, beckons.

"Come with me," she says in a thick accent. "I am Doctor Aashi Jani, the resident on call today. Please leave your belongings here. We are trying to keep the room as sterile as possible."

She must sense my uneasiness about handing over my treasures. "They will be safe," she assures me.

She leads me through a set of extra-wide wooden doors into a long corridor of glaring white. Shiny chrome handrails flow along the length of the walls, except for the evenly spaced gaps of each room's doorway.

Reaching the old man's room, the doctor stops. "He is suffering tremendous chest pain. I have him on intravenous medication to suppress it, somewhat. It's only temporary, only for his sake of comfort."

"I was told this was dire."

"Yes, it is. Apparently, he has a history of heart disease. There is much damage to the organ. His pain is most likely linked to some issue with perfusion. When someone experiences decreased blood flow, this can be quite dangerous, as the tissues in the body can be quickly damaged by its restriction."

A nurse approaches us. She extends a clipboard, containing several papers, to the doctor. The doctor automatically draws a pen from her coat pocket and scribbles several times.

"When he was brought into Emergency," she continues, "triage results indicated he had decreased perfusion."

"How bad is he? How much time does he have?"

"I must be honest. I have little hope he will see the sunrise tomorrow, Mister Christian. My inconclusive prognosis is he suffers from advanced atherosclerotic renal artery stenosis. His condition, along with his medical history and his unwholesome lifestyle, is working against him as we speak. I have him scheduled for a procedure, an angioplasty, if he makes it through the night. He's conscious but very weak. Fifteen minutes," she says, twisting her wrist to animate observance of her watch.

She lowers her chin, while keeping her eyes fixed in a piercing gaze, like a mother giving direction to a child. "Fifteen minutes and no more," she reiterates as she and the nurse continue down the hall to assess some other ailing soul.

The impersonal honesty, the coldness of reality, a

feeling of complete hopelessness looms over this dreadful situation. *Every moment of life is valuable,* I think. *What value can I add to this old man's final moments? Why did he summon me? What does he expect?* I take a deep breath.

As the door slowly closes behind me, I move to the bedside where the old man, connected to life through tubes and wires, lies motionless under a thin, gray blanket. Medical devices surround him beeping and blinking simultaneously.

"Christian," he whispers in a soft, raspy voice, "is that you?"

"Yes, it's me," I say as I grasp his cold, frail hand. "I thought you were sleeping."

"No. I just didn't want to watch the light fade, alone."

"Well, you are not alone now, I'm here. Open your eyes."

"I'm glad you came, Christian. I needed to talk to . . . well, you. I have little time left for confessions. What good are they now anyway? I can't undo past indiscretions. I have been a thoughtless, selfish bastard my whole life. There's no room for me in Valhalla, I know that."

"Let's not talk about that just yet. You still have time."

"No, no . . . I was a terrible man and a worse father," he says with labored breath. "I missed so much in life because of stupid choices, bad choices. Missed being with a woman I truly loved . . . ruined her life, and my son's . . . I missed every birthday . . . did you know that? Every single one."

"Don't be so hard on yourself. We've all made choices we regret. This is not a time to focus on what you didn't do, rather on what you did do. I'm sure there must be some choice you made along the way that you are thankful for, something you are proud of."

"Well . . . there is something, I guess. Christian, now I know why I wanted you here. I need you to do something for me. Please, Christian, tell my son, tell Antton I didn't miss everything."

"Wouldn't you rather tell him yourself? Father to son?"

"No . . . no . . . It's better this way. I don't want him to see me like this. When the doctor gave us the prognosis this morning, I made him leave and promise not to come back until it's over. We both know it won't be long. We've said our goodbyes."

"If you're sure."

"I'm sure. I don't think I could tell him to his face anyway. You understand?"

"Sure, old man, I understand. What is it you want to tell him?"

"Tell him I didn't miss everything," he says struggling with every breath. "I did see him one time when he was a young man. You see, I learned he was graduating, with honors, from the academy. I saved some money to buy a ticket to his graduation. Didn't have enough for a proper suit, but I wore the best clothes I had. I sat in the back, out of the way. Guess I looked out of place though because some of the guards questioned me, asked me to show them my ticket. I was so proud to show them and tell them who I was. They asked me if I wanted to sit closer so he could see me . . . they didn't understand. When it was all over, I heard people talking about Antton and how he had turned out to be such a fine man. I was so very proud."

"You didn't go talk to him . . . let him know you were there?"

"No . . . no. I didn't want to get in the way. It was his day, not mine. Hell, he didn't even know who I was. It was better to leave things the way they were. I still don't understand why he looked for me after all those years. Probably just wanted to watch me die."

"You couldn't be more wrong, old man. He's your son, he loves you."

"Love? Why would he love me? I never did anything good for him . . . never."

"Simply because he is your son. And, you will always be his father."

For a moment, only the beeping of the machines fills the silence.

"I fear I am fading away with no place to go," he says, as his breathing becomes even more slow and shallow.

The door to the room gently swings opens. Only a silhouette of the nurse is visible. "Your fifteen minutes are almost over," she warns.

"One more minute." I beg.

She steps out, closing the door.

"Christian, I'm afraid," the old man whispers to me. "My life turned out nothing like I had hoped or imagined and now the clock is winding down."

"Don't talk like that."

"It's true. I feel it. Only a minute more before time

stands still for me. No rewinding."

"Then live it the way you imagine."

"The way I imagine?"

"Like Shakespeare said: The world is your stage. Do you remember the Tempest, a scene where Prospero's wand is broken?"

The old man's eyes become narrow as he stares beyond me, across the room.

"And his words. Remember his words. '*We are such stuff as dreams are made on, and our little life is rounded with a sleep.*' Do you remember that?"

"You are wise," he whispers. "Yes! A dream to help me cross the darkened waters of the sea, into the shadows of the distant mist. I will be captain of my own ship."

"Yes, your very own vessel. A three-masted barque sailing the Mediterranean with the wind at your back. Clear blue skies to the horizon."

"I see it! I see white-crested waves cascading all around. And sailors—there are plenty on the deck."

"Yes! And men on the sails, fore and aft! All at your command."

"Yes, I see it. I feel the sun warm on my face. I shall sail onward . . . onward . . . to a new sea. Onward to the great un . . . "

His grip fades as he heaves a heavy sigh.

"Christian," he mumbles. "Tell my son I'm proud of him. Tell him I am thankful he found me. Tell him I love him . . . I will dream now." The old man's eyes close; his hand falls from mine to his side.

"Valhalla is before you, Izaro. Indeed, the Great God

Odin smiles." I whisper in his ear as his body releases him to peace.

No words are spoken as I exit past the nurse who has just returned to remind me my fifteen minutes has expired. I walk the sterile hallway to a waiting area where I see the captain pacing back and forth.

"He is at peace now. Odin has ushered him to Valhalla." I say. "Join me in the chapel for a while?"

"No, Christian. I'm not really a . . . "

"Everyone believes in something, Captain."

We walk together to a small room, furnished with modest decoration and basic seating. At the front, there is a padded rail for kneeling in prayer, above which hangs a painting of a stained-glass window. A small box mounted near the door to our right is labeled with a plastic engraved sign that says, 'Donations.' In unison, we migrate to a couple of chairs near the entrance.

"You know, Christian, I have seen good men die in battle. I have seen others die by the hands of their own fellow citizens. I watched my own wife and my mother fade from this world: somehow this is different. I certainly did not think I would feel such strong emotion for that grumpy old bastard I knew so little of. There was a time I felt such hatred toward him, even wanted to take revenge if I ever found him. Then, after all those years, when I finally discovered his whereabouts, when I realized what a miserable life he had lived . . . "

"Forgiveness and compassion should always trump revenge and hate. You are an exceptional man, Captain: everything you did for him. A lesser man wouldn't have forgiven him, and certainly wouldn't have taken him in as you did."

"Still, it is a strange feeling. He was not the best of men, but he was my father."

"I think the bond between father and son is a mystery we will never unravel . . . You know . . . my father died when I was a young man; I was only in my twenties. Even though he was always home, I never got to know him. We were like strangers living under the same roof. God, I don't even know if I liked him. Still, when he died . . . "

"Christian, I see you and I as some sort of brothers, part of some greater defined community, part of the main. You might think you do not need anyone, however, I am very glad to have met you. I think I needed to have you here."

"I may have been too hasty in my view about Donne. I am beginning to understand your perspective, Captain. Reading the manuscript my wife left for me was very enlightening."

"Yes, the manuscript. Did it have an alternate ending as we supposed?"

"Actually, it ended quite dramatically different than Bishop Rutter's official version. It was all about acceptance and forgiveness. In my opinion, it had a better ending, one that would have molded civilization, all of mankind, to be more understanding of other cultures, religions, and the communities in which we cohabitate. There would probably be more compassion in today's world if that would have been the official version instead of Rutter's hate and vengeance spin. At least I'd like to think so."

"Interesting. I believe I would like to read that ballad someday. And your wife. You have never spoken of the circumstances that actually brought you on this adventure. All I know is what Mercher shared yesterday about her being here on a dig. I sense there is a lot more to it, something unpleasant from what I gather. I am quite a good listener, if you would like to share."

"Well," I begin slowly. "A couple of years ago, my wife, Lottie, began to have trouble with her eye: just her right eye. It was very painful for her and kept getting worse. We went to three different ophthalmologists, the family practitioner, Ear, Nose, and Throat specialists, even a neurologist. No one could figure out why she was having such pain. The best guess was a simple condition called 'Dry Eye.' So, they gave her all kinds of prescriptions, however, none of the medications helped. We vowed we would keep researching until we discovered something, but her condition never improved."

"And you tried everything?"

"Yes. Over the counter drops, prescription medications, holistic remedies. We never thought it could be from a tumor."

"A tumor?"

"When she arrived on the Island, she started having worse pain so she decided to have some tests done here: CAT scan, blood work. That's when they discovered the tumor."

"Were they able to remove it? Or shrink it with radiation therapy?"

"No. She chose against having surgery, chemo, or the therapy."

"What? Why?"

"Well, she was so disheartened with the inexactness of the prognosis. They couldn't say for certain that any of it would cure her. She struggled with the emotional drain and expense of unsuccessful remedies. She said she didn't want to waste, to squander our savings trying to live one more day just to avoid the inevitable. I still question whether it was the right choice, if there was something more I could have done."

"How long has it been?"

A gentle rap at the door interrupts our conversation. It is Mercher.

"May I join you?" he asks.

"The captain's father passed away a short while ago," I inform him.

"Oh dear. My sincerest condolences, Captain."

As Mercher settles in, another knock is heard at the door. This time it is the nurse.

"Gentlemen," she addresses us. "Captain," she says, looking directly at him.

"Yes?"

"We need you to come to the nurse's station, sir. The doctor would like to speak with you."

"Yes, of course."

"There is something before you go, Captain. Something the old man, I mean, your father, made me promise to tell you."

"Yes, Christian, what is it?"

"He wanted you to know he didn't miss everything. He told me he was there when you graduated from the academy."

"I do not understand?"

"He saved money for a ticket: made the trip. He watched from the back of the field, out of the way."

"Why did he not introduce himself, tell me who he was? Why did he never mention it all this time?"

"Part of the mystery between fathers and sons I guess. Seems men, in general, at least in my experience, are uncomfortable sharing our true feelings with those we cherish most. Your father wanted you to know how proud he was that day, for what a good man you became in spite of him abandoning you. He asked me to tell you he was thankful you found him, and that he loved you."

"Thank you, Christian. I am indeed glad you were here," he says shaking my hand. Exiting the chapel with the nurse, the captain torpidly follows her down the hall.

Mercher and I stare blankly around the room for a moment, uneasy with the solemnness of the situation.

Mercher eventually pipes up. "I contacted the catalog department about the original manuscript Elan was supposed to have delivered. They said they have not received anything yet. It is very concerning. You see, Mister Christian, possession of an uncatalogued ancient manuscript carries with it severe penalties on this Island."

"Really? I didn't know that."

"Moreover, those who conspire, whether knowingly or unknowingly, are charged as accessories. I do hope Elan has not forgotten that. Now if you will excuse me I need to call my office and check on a pressing matter. I will meet you at the nurse's station when you are ready. No hurry my good man."

Sitting in solitude, I look at the painting of the stained-glass window. The bottom panel depicts the birth of Christ, the middle the sermon on the mount, and the top is of the crucifixion. Around the outer edge and winding between the three panels are different sizes and colors of geometrical shapes. *We are born into this world, we travel life's path, and then we die. The path, the choices we make along the way; that is the important part,* I think to myself.

"Mister Christian," the same nurse from before calls from the chapel entrance. "Pardon me, sir, I hope I am not interrupting. The resident oncologist has a package for you at the front desk. She requests a brief consultation with you, if you have time."

"The oncologist? Yes, of course, thank you. I'll be right there."

An elderly volunteer sitting behind the nurse's desk sees me approaching. She adjusts her gold-rimmed glasses as she reads the label on the envelope. "Mister Christian?"

"Yes."

"The results of your wife's tests, the second opinion verification," she says extending the packet toward me. "The doctor will be with you shortly. You can have a seat over there if you'd like to review the contents."

I settle in a comfortable chair and begin pulling various reports from the envelope. Before I get a chance to review the many forms, a small framed woman with silky black hair comes over to me.

"Mister Christian, Hi. I'm Doctor Balakrish, the resident oncologist."

I rise to greet her.

"So glad to meet you. We wanted to make sure you received your wife's test results before you left. We tried to call her with the news, however, the number doesn't seem to be correct. We were ready to mail them, then the nurse overhead a conversation between one of our patients and his son, a sea captain I believe, who mentioned you by name so we thought this might be faster."

"Yes. I'm here to gather my wife's things and take them home. I met Captain Aiza and his father on the trip over."

"Have you reviewed the test results?"

"No, I was just getting ready to."

"Well the news is good. Very good."

"What?"

"Yes, the test results revealed her tumor is not malignant."

"I don't understand. The last we heard it was, and had the potential to metastasize."

"That was a preliminary test. The secondary tests ruled out malignancy. Her condition is still going to be painful, but her outlook is very good."

"But, we thought . . . she thought, it was pretty final."

"No, no, this test from hematology confirms no malignant cells."

"I . . . she . . . "

"Are you okay, Mister Christian?"

"I feel ... "

Suddenly, all I see are waves of indistinguishable shapes flashing around me. I hear only muffled voices as if my head is under water. The doctor places one hand on my arm and leans into me with her shoulder lowering my limp frame back into the chair.

Gradually, sounds become normal again and the flashing subsides. Now, the elderly volunteer is standing next to me offering a drink of water from a paper cup. I look at the doctor. "Her tumor is benign?"

"Yes. It is not that common, yet it is not unheard of either. There are patients just like her, who live with this kind of growth and have no additional problems. There's no reason to think she won't live a long healthy life. The biggest thing will be the pain. She will need to figure out what works best for her. Your family doctor, or possibly her ophthalmologist, should be able to assist with that."

"I ... we had no idea, we both thought ... "

"You will talk to her. Give her the good news?"

"Yes, of course. I'll call her as soon as I get back to the hotel."

"Best of luck to you and your wife. Tell her I said, 'hello'."

"Thank you. I will. I can't tell you how happy I am. I just wish I could get home sooner. The boat ride back to Liverpool tomorrow evening will seem like forever. What great news, Doctor. Thank you again!"

After the doctor leaves, the volunteer informs me Mercher received a call and had to leave unexpectedly.

"He asked me to call for a car when you are ready."

I assume the captain is occupied, addressing final arrangements for the old man and my business here is complete, so I thank her, and ask her to call for a car.

A few minutes later I am snugly in the back of a cab, only slightly damp from dashing through the ever-insistent downpour to get to the car. Descending the hill into the city, the young taxi driver tries to invoke polite conversation to no avail. Anxious to make the call and prepare for my departure tomorrow, my mind is busy with other things. *I have the test results, I have the manuscript at the hotel. Oh no! The cylinder and satchel, I forgot them at the hospital, but I will have time to retrieve them first thing in the morning. Right now, I really need to make that call.* Reaching our destination, the young man jumps out and opens my door.

Generously paying the fare, I tell him, "Keep the change."

"Thank you, sir," he replies with a big toothy grin. "Thanks a lot!" He hurriedly slides back into the driver's seat and pulls away.

The faithful workhorse, tram in tow, clops along the road past me, this time he is covered in a wool blanket to shield him from the rain.

As I enter the lobby, Mary, the hostess I met only this morning, is dusting around little vases of flowers on the window sills, her back to the door. I try to clear my throat quietly to gain her attention, nevertheless the sound catches her unaware causing her to jerk.

"Oh, good afternoon Mister . . . " she says, patting her

lips with her finger. It's clear she remembers me, but is having trouble recalling my name.

"Christian," I remind her.

"Oh yes, Mister Christian!"

I notice she has removed the apron from this morning and added a white pearl necklace complementing her blue flowery dress. Across the room through the doorway to the pub, I see a familiar face.

"Excuse me, Mary. I believe I know that person."

"Oh yes, yes. I remember now. I was supposed to tell you a man from the ship is waiting for you in the lounge."

"Thank you."

"Oh, and housekeeping is done with your room too. Let me know if you need any . . . " Her words trail off as I join Cook at the bar.

Today, instead of his uniform of white, he is wearing a long gray coat, black jeans, and boots. As I approach, I see he has both hands wrapped tightly around a tankard of beer.

"I heard about the old man," he says in a very somber tone.

"Already? That was quick."

"Small island."

"I guess so."

"We may've had our differences, me and the old man, but we were both sailors and that made us brothers of the sea. Too bad I won't get to hear him bitchin' at me no more. I'll miss that for sure."

"I believe he was a good man at heart. Seems he just made some choices he regretted."

"He was all right, the old bastard. Don't matter anyway. He's gone now. How's the captain takin' it?"

"He's pretty upset, more so than I thought he would be. He really cared for the old man, loved him even."

"We all did." Cook says staring into his beer. "Well, uh, I just wanted to say thanks for looking after him the other day. And, uh, it was good to meet you."

Cook finishes the last swig of his beer and places his mug on the counter. Tossing a few pounds down, he slips off his stool, and escapes out the door. Just then Maggie emerges from the kitchen. She scoops the money and tankard up with one hand, wiping the counter with her other.

"Have a drink on me, Christian. Looks like you could use one," she says, pouring a fresh cold Stella. "And I have a warm pie on the way."

"Thank you, Maggie, but I really need to make a telephone call."

"It's okay. Take the beer with you and I'll have mum bring the pie up in a minute."

"That's very kind. I'll take you up on that."

I climb the stairs, fueled only by adrenaline. Reaching my room, I take a big gulp from the mug, go straight to the telephone, and dial. I can't wait to tell Lottie the good news. "Please answer, please," I whisper. As the ringing continues, "I just want to hear your sweet voice."

Several rings later, the answering machine connects and I can only leave a message. Explaining in detail the conversation with the doctor and how happy I am, I end my message, saying, "I love you Lottie . . . I always have, and I always will."

Placing the receiver back on its base, I wonder why she didn't answer. The clock on the wall catches my eye as I take another sip. I calculate the time difference. *It's Thursday, she's probably just out with her friend Debbie.* I try to calm myself. *I'll call again first thing in the morning.*

Content in the chair, cold beer in hand, I reminisce about the day's events. A soft knock at the door startles me just enough to make me jerk; a bit of Stella dribbles down my shirt.

"Mister Christian?" I hear Mary's muffled voice on the other side. "I've got a warm pie and another lager for you."

"Coming," I say, chuckling to myself. I startled her earlier. Now, she has returned the favor.

"You must have had quite a big day," she says as she places the items on the table beside the chair.

"Thank you, Mary. Sorry for the trouble."

"Oh, it's no bother," she smiles sweetly, as she gently closes the door behind her.

Hot cheesy deliciousness and ice-cold beer satisfies my hunger. Savoring every buttery crumb, then gulping the last swig from the mug, my senses return and I feel almost normal again. The anguish and despair experienced over the past week finally melts away, replaced by relief and tranquility. My journey has been so much more successful than I ever dreamt. I cannot wait to be with her again: to hold her.

I begin preparing for the trip home. *I have the wonderful test results. I have the manuscript . . . Where's the book?* I think. *That's odd.* I scan the table where I left the swapped manuscript this morning; only the lamp and dirty dishes are there now. *I know it was right there when Mercher and I left this morning. Where could it have gone?*

I decide to return the dishes to the bar and see if Mary or Maggie can check with housekeeping. Perhaps they removed it thinking it was part of the hotel's collection. I realize it was only Lottie's draft sketches, still, who would have taken it?

"Well I can't imagine." Mary says when I inquire. "Let me summon the cleaning lady and we can ask her. She's new, but she's usually very thorough. Such a nice girl too. Does a really good job."

Momentarily, a young woman wearing a plain gray dress with a black collar and bulky white shoes appears. Her round face has a sweet expression. She twitches with a look of total confusion as Mary inquires about the book.

"He says it was very old, leather cover and bound with twine."

"I didn't see one, ma'am."

"Would you have moved it when you were dusting things?"

"No ma'am. I remember, Mister Christian's room was very clean, didn't even need to make the bed. Looked like it hadn't even been slept in."

"He says it was on the table by the chair. Are you sure you didn't see it?"

"No ma'am, just the lamp and a water glass. I put a clean glass back on the nightstand when I poured fresh water in the pitcher. All due respect ma'am. I didn't see no book."

Her innocence is evident.

"Thank you for your time, miss. Sorry to be a bother," I tell her. "I'm sure it will turn up."

"Yes, I guess we better let you get back to work now," Mary adds.

"Just one thing, ma'am. Not sure it's important, but there was a man here, earlier. Not one of your guests I mean."

"A man? What did he look like?" I ask.

"He was kinda oldish. Looked smart, ya know? Sorta nervous fella. Seemed to be in a real hurry."

"What was he doing?"

"Well, he just rushed passed me on the staircase. I was goin' up and he was goin' down."

"Is that all you remember?" I ask.

"Well, he seemed real polite. Said 'excuse me' when he passed."

"Thank you again," I say, as I recall Mercher's earlier words. His warning. His threat. Was it him? I thank Mary for her assistance and return to my room. I open the secret compartment in the bottom of my overnight bag and retrieve the binder containing the original manuscript. By morning Mercher will suspect, will know what I have done, but I do not regret it. Reading this ancient story helped me understand so much of what Lottie was trying to tell me about people, about change, about choices, about life: about us. Tomorrow, I will do the right thing and somehow return this to Elan before he gets in trouble. Hopefully, he can make it right with Mercher.

Daylight has once again been swallowed by darkness. Calm and content for the first time since this journey began, I close the drapes, dress for bed, and collapse into the comfort of down-filled blankets. I lie on my back staring at the ceiling thinking of her and how happy she will be when she checks the answering machine. Peacefully dreaming of us together again, I drift into a deep slumber.

Chapter Five

Peeking through early morning haze, streaks of sunlight creep around the edge of the drapes, casting odd shadows in my room. The storm has passed. I waken refreshed, anxious with desire to begin the day and start my voyage home. I shuffle to the bathroom. My arthritic fingers struggle to open the small travel bag. After generously applying shaving gel to help the razor glide gently over this uneven terrain, I methodically move the razor across my face: first left, then right, then down. As I step into the shower, steam fills the small room like a dense fog. I cannot help but dream of her again. This time; however, the vision is different. I am home with her again, holding her in my arms, celebrating the good news.

Dressed for the day, however, not ready to depart for a few hours, I decide to put in a call to the university's local office. Elan is not in yet, so I leave a message asking him to meet me at the hotel as soon as possible. I request the receptionist write 'URGENT' on the note, sure he will understand. Picking up the receiver to call Lottie, I realize she will be sound asleep at this hour. *I'll try again later before I leave to board the ship*, I think.

"Happy Saint Patrick's Day," Mary's sweet voice greets me as I enter the foyer.

"Good morning, Mary. I will be checking out later today, but I have some things to take care of before I go."

"Okay, I'll have your charges calculated whenever you

are ready. It's been a pleasure to have you with us, Mister Christian."

The familiar aroma of roasted coffee and fresh pastries tease my senses.

"First, I think I'll get some coffee, Mary," I say as I head to the lounge. I hear the lyrics to the song, 'Autumn Leaves'. It's one of Lottie's favorites. I remember how she would point it out to me every time she heard it playing on the radio. It is a sad tune, albeit, very romantic. I know that is why she likes it. She has a very tender-hearted soul, always tearing up at romantic movies and songs like this.

Maggie has just finished making a Bloody Mary for a familiar looking gent perched on one of the stools.

"Gil?" I say as I approach.

His big furry face wrinkles as he squints at me. Then, his eyes widen, lips parting widely revealing pearly white teeth below his thick mustache.

"Christian!" he says as he extends his hand. We shake like two old friends reuniting after a long time apart.

"Gil the hopeful romantic. How are you?"

"I'm well. Happy Saint Patrick's Day to you! Today, I will claim to be Irish!"

"Ha! Thanks! You too."

"Join me for a Bloody Mary? I'm sure Maggie would be happy to mix one up for you, wouldn't you my dear girl?"

"Sure. Be happy to. Just give me a sec," she says.

"Thanks Maggie," I say.

"Ah, what a week, well last few days, it has been," Gil sighs happily.

"I must agree."

"Right, yes. Were you able to accomplish all you planned? Did you gather your wife's belongings?"

"Yes, I did. And more."

"Really? Do tell."

"Oh, I'm not sure you would be interested. It's just something she left for me to read."

"If it's a mushy love letter, you can spare me the details. I do, however, enjoy a good book now and again."

"Well then, you might like this. When I arrived, I was given an ancient manuscript. Lottie, that's my wife's name, left it for me. She had read it while she was here and wanted me to read it so I would understand some things she had been trying to tell me. It was very enlightening."

"Really? Ancient manuscript you say?"

"Yes, a written account of the ballad of Fin and Oshin. It's pretty obscure. Not sure you . . . "

"I know that story. It's a very well-known ballad of Celtic mythology. That's the one where the village girls tie this fellow Gorry to the ground and burn his feet. He then seeks revenge and burns their homes. Then Fin, Gorry's rival, seeks revenge on him and has Gorry drawn and quartered. Right?"

"Well, yes, actually. I mean that is the way Bishop Rutter's official written version goes. The one my wife left for me had a very different ending though. It was found during the excavation of Rutter's tomb; it had been buried with him."

"Different you say? Right, well . . . that is very

interesting. Between you and me, I've never agreed with the ending Rutter transcribed."

"So, you've read the ballad?"

"Right, yes, several years ago I read Rutter's account anyway. You say the one you have is different? Just curious, how does it end?"

Maggie delivers my Bloody Mary. "Ah, the ancient book again. Did you read it?" she asks. "How did it end? Was it different like you anticipated?"

"Well, yes, significantly. Instead of revenge perpetuating revenge, in the end, Fin and the villagers search for Gorry to forgive him."

Just then a middle-aged couple enter and seat themselves at a table by the window.

"That sounds way better to me," Maggie says. "Excuse me gents, duty calls. I never get to hear the whole of anything!" she remarks, as she leaves us to serve her new customers.

"She's right, that ending does sound better and more plausible, in my opinion," Gil says.

"What do you mean?"

"Imagine, Christian, when man first wrote history from oral stories like this ancient ballad. Imagine the power to write as he chose. Free to manipulate facts to support the ending others are meant to accept and believe."

"That's exactly what some of us were debating the other afternoon, before I read the ballad. A couple of us felt, well we agreed, it could benefit certain political or religious groups, if the outcome of written ballads supported their beliefs, encouraging their way of thinking. It could influence the way humankind, the way society, evolved."

"That's spot on, Christian. Exactly right!"

"What did you mean when you said you never believed Bishop Rutter's official version? This fellow I met, Mister Mercher, alluded to that as well. He said there were rumors Rutter embellished most of his writings, but he emphatically discounted them as unsubstantiated? Now I think that may have been because he is a direct descendant."

"Well, you see, the thing is, during Early Medieval times, the Dark Ages, when this ballad would have been recited, there was in place, the Senchus Mor. Ancient Celtic law from the Brehon."

"Celtic law?"

"Right, yes, Well, the people living on the Island at that time, around the thirteenth century, were a diverse group of Danes, Normans, Celts, Druids, and Christians, all with their own beliefs, traditions, and social constructs. However, even though multiple political and religious changes were evolving throughout society, Brehon law remained intact for several more centuries. It was a civil-based legal system, requiring a similar form of repayment for an act committed."

"So, the legal system of that age wouldn't have allowed such harsh degree of retribution for the crime Gorry committed?"

"That's right. Like I said even though the feudal system was introduced around that period, Brehon laws were most commonly practiced, lasting until, well practically the middle of the seventeenth century. The Brehon were judges, arbitrators, concerned mostly with like payment, compensation, for harm done, not having someone drawn and quartered for goodness sake!"

"So, the people would have never . . . "

"Very improbable. From what you have told me, I believe the manuscript you are in possession of is a more accurate account of the ancient ballad. The ending is certainly more appropriate to the cultural norms practiced during that time."

"Well, Gil, you certainly seem very knowledgeable on the topic. If I might ask, what made you read Rutter's version? I had never even heard of the ballad until Lottie wrote me about it. I mean it's certainly not on the best-sellers list. Are you a history buff or something?"

"Well, Christian, to you I may appear to be a lonely old pensioner trying to find the next chapter of his life, however, my retirement began only after a long tenure as professor emeritus for the school of Cultural and Historical Studies at the University of Sydney."

"Really? That's quite impressive. Should I call you Doctor Gil?"

"No, no. Please, just Gil. Say, Christian, do you think it would it be possible for me to read your copy of the ballad? I would like very much to compare the two."

"Sorry, I really can't. You see, it's not a copy. It is the original. The young man that gave it to me wanted to make sure I read the exact version Lottie did. She made him promise. So, he didn't send it through the Office of

Archives for review and copying. He was afraid parts would be redacted if he did."

"Oh . . . I see. You know, Christian, this young man could get in a lot of trouble for what he has done. There are laws . . . "

"I know. Mister Mercher warned me of the seriousness yesterday. I need to get the manuscript back to him, Elan, so he can route it through the proper channels. I called the university first thing and left an urgent, albeit cryptic, message for him. I asked him to meet me here this morning."

"I do hope for his sake he takes care of this as soon as possible."

After taking a few more sips of our Bloody Marys, I ask, "So, Gil, how goes your romantic quest?"

"Good, very good indeed. I still have trouble grasping the concept of a soul mate, though. I don't believe there are pairs across the world destined to bump into each other. However, I am starting to see your point. Maybe, just maybe, once you find somebody who is right for you, your love can last forever. Even if you're away from each other for a very long time."

I follow his gaze across the room. Mary is standing at the lobby desk.

"That's Mary," he says.

"Oh, I know, I met her yesterday. She is a sweet woman."

"You don't understand, Christian, that is my Mary," he says grinning from sideburn to sideburn.

"No ... Really? That's great! So that means Maggie ... "

"Yep!"

"Wow! You have had quite an exciting few days."

"A good man, very recently, told me having a soul mate is not bells ringing and birds chirping, it's a choice you make. You know, once you commit, your partner becomes your soul mate. Well, Christian, I'm planning to commit to my Mary, if she'll have me."

"Good for you, Gil. I wish you the best of luck."

Just then, the captain enters the lobby in full regalia. "Good morning," he greets us as he approaches the bar through the double doors.

"Good morning, Captain," I say. "Gil, this is Captain Aiza, from the ship. Captain, this is Gil, a fellow traveler I met on the voyage over."

"Right, yes, I thought you looked familiar, Captain. Nice to meet you."

"Good to meet you. Gil, was it?"

"That's right. Now, if you gentlemen will excuse me, there is lovely lady I need to speak to. Glad we bumped into one another again, Christian." Gil puts his empty glass on the counter and exits in Mary's direction.

"My friend, the nurse you left these with yesterday asked me to deliver them to you," the captain says, as he hands me the cylinder and the satchel I had forgotten at the hospital. "She said you rushed off without them."

"I appreciate the delivery, Captain. I thought I would have to hire a car this morning to go get them."

"No trouble at all. That is why I dropped them off. I did not want you to worry about them all day. I heard you will be sailing back as far as Liverpool with us this evening?"

"Yes, I had to cancel the return leg when I missed my flight over. Quite a mix-up. My flight from there to the States is still confirmed though."

"Very good. I look forward to another enlightening conversation on the voyage back. Christian, I do hope the time you spent with my father was not an inconvenience to you."

"Not at all. I am glad to have met him. Will you be taking him back with you?"

"No. I have decided to donate his organs to the local university. I hope it will help someone else somehow, maybe even afford another more time."

"I think that's a very noble decision. My wife and I both plan to donate our remains to science, when the time comes."

"It was just so sudden. If we could have had a little longer . . .If. . .If I would have known. . ."

"I understand how you feel, but none of us ever know. The only thing we know with certainty is, well . . . from the moment life begins, death is its inevitable end. The mystery for each of us, a fear we all share, is how and when. I think all any of us can do is make the most of the time we have. Make the best choices we can. Choices we can be proud of as we navigate our path through life."

"Yes, Christian, I guess you are right about that. Well my friend, I must get to the ship and prepare for our voyage. I will see you there this evening. We have a bottle of Jameson to finish."

"See you there, Captain."

Slinging the satchel over my shoulder and grabbing

the cylinder in my left hand, I walk toward the stairs. Gil and Mary are staring across the front desk at each other, like two love-struck teenagers. As I walk past them, Gil notices something fall from the satchel.

"Christian, a moment," he says. "I believe this fell from your bag."

He hands me a folded piece of paper with what look to be handwritten notes.

"Thanks," I say, unfolding it. A pressed yellow rose falls out and lands on the floor at my feet. Reading what is scrawled on the page before me, I realize, these are not notes rather a letter Lottie must have written before departing.

John,

My dear wonderful husband; love of my life. You know me so well. Only you know how my spirit has been tested through the years by illnesses, broken bones, and the many surgeries. It has always been one more thing on top of one more thing. I guess I should say 'our' spirit, because every time you were right by my side, nursing me, encouraging me: always so compassionate, so caring, so loving. It must have taken a lot to always be the strong one. Words cannot describe how grateful I am for our time together, we really made the most of it, you and me. Just two young kids making our way through this crazy world. I want you to know you gave me the best life any woman could have. So much of who I am, what I have accomplished, is only because of you and your selflessness. This time, this time, my darling man, I fear our souls have been challenged with such intensity it is smothering the joy of all the years past.

Only your endless compassion has carried me this far in our current relentless battle: one I'm afraid I am getting too tired to fight.

I hope you read the book. I hope you understand what it meant to me, about you, about us, and what I have chosen to do. Please don't be mad or hurt. I planned it this way. You know, while you're over there collecting my things. It is why I made you go. I love you John. I always have and I always will . . . Sorry my love, I fear you will have to finish our rhyme on your own. I know you will choose the perfect ending.

Yours eternally,

Lottie

Panic stricken, I drop the paper to the floor on top of the rose. Mary comes around the desk and retrieves both. As she begins to read, I dash up the stairs to my room and scramble to the telephone. My fingers fumble to dial. No answer. Eight rings. Only the answering machine, again.

"Sweetie, don't . . . I found your letter! Please don't do anything! Listen to all the messages please! The results from the tests were good! I will be home as soon as I can! We have more time!"

I drop the receiver back on its base and sit there, on the edge of the bed, stunned, drained, helpless.

A moment later, Mary and Gil are standing in the open doorway of my room.

"Christian, is there anything we can do?" Gil asks.

"We read the letter," Mary says. "I'm so sorry."

"Please. I need to pack. I need to figure something out, something quicker."

"I'll get your ledger ready. I'm truly sorry, Mister Christian," Mary says as she leaves, laying the letter and rose on the table.

"Right, yes, well Christian, I'm sure you will find all is well when you return," Gil says, trying to calm me. "Her love for you will prevail. It will keep her strong until you arrive. I'm sure of it."

"Thanks Gil, I hope you're right. I do hope you're right."

"If there is anything I can do . . ."

"Thanks Gil," I say, as I hastily shove my belongings into my overnight bag. I notice the manuscript. "Gil, there is something."

"Yes?"

"It's the manuscript. Could you protect it, give it to Elan, for me? I wouldn't ask, but it is important. In case he doesn't get here before I leave. I don't want the kid to suffer any repercussions for doing what he thought was right."

"Don't give it another thought. I'll be happy to."

Just then the telephone rings. Heart pounding, I rush to pick up the receiver hoping it will be her. "Hello! Sweetie?"

"No . . . Mister Christian. This is Doctor Balakrish. We met yesterday."

"Oh, yes, Doctor. Is there something I can do for you?"

"Actually, there might be something I can do for you. Yesterday you said you wanted to get home as soon as possible, but you had to wait for the boat ride back to Liverpool."

"Yes, that's right."

"Well, if your schedule is flexible, we have a medical flight leaving Ronaldsway for Liverpool later this morning. There will be one seat available next to the pilot if you want it. I can make the arrangements."

"Want it? Yes! Thank you. What time does it leave?"

"Around eleven o'clock. We are transporting a patient over for a medical procedure we don't perform here. Fairly routine. I just didn't know about it yesterday when we spoke."

"Thank you, Doctor! I will arrange for a car. I will be there! Thank you! Thank you for everything!"

"Safe travels, Mister Christian. Glad I could help."

"Gil, great news! There is a medical flight leaving for Liverpool at eleven o'clock. It will save so much time. I'm going to call and see if I can get an earlier flight back to Charlotte. Wish me luck."

"Right, yes. Of course! Good Luck! I'll wait for you downstairs."

After successfully rescheduling my ticket from Liverpool to Charlotte, I descend the staircase, luggage in hand. As I reach the bottom, I see Elan standing with Gil near the front door. I hurriedly approach them.

"So glad you made it before I left, Elan. I see Gil delivered the manuscript."

"Yes, sir. Thank you for leaving the message. I was beginning to wonder how I was going to smooth things over with Mercher. It's a bigger deal than I thought. He told me yesterday if the original didn't arrive in his office 'very soon' he would have to start an investigation."

"I know, I know. I'm so sorry if this causes any trouble for you. I am glad you gave me the original, though. I fear a redacted version would not have been so enlightening. Gil, Elan, thank you both. Now I need to call for a car. I'll have just enough time to swing by the harbor to let Captain Aiza know I will not be sailing back with him. He'll have to drink the Jameson alone, I guess. Unless you are sailing back, Gil?"

"No, no. I'll be staying a while longer. I have things to attend to here," he says looking over at Mary.

"Mister Christian, I'd be happy to drive you to the harbor and airport," Elan says. "I dropped Vikki off at the site earlier. She knows I was coming here and then to see Mister Mercher to try and explain things. She said she won't need me until the end of the day. I could give you a lift on my way to see Mercher if you like. It's no bother."

"Really? That would be great! Thank you! I just need to settle my charges with Mary."

"I'll wait for you in the jeep, sir."

"Okay! Be right out."

My account settled, and goodbyes exchanged with Mary, Maggie, and Gil, I find myself in the jeep racing along the promenade to the port. Elan pulls up directly alongside the ship. The captain is standing on deck. As I approach the gangplank, I shout to him.

"Permission to come aboard, Captain?"

He nods and motions permission.

Sparkles of brilliant light flicker on the placid waters of the bay as a warm gentle breeze, much different than that during our arrival, pleasantly wafts past.

"Captain, I just came to tell you I've been offered a plane ride back to Liverpool. It leaves at eleven o'clock. I was able to get an earlier flight home to Charlotte, too. I need to get home. I need to be with my wife."

"I understand, Christian. It was a pleasure to meet you. And I am ever grateful for the compassion you showed my father. You are welcome to sail with me anytime."

"Thank you. I am grateful for your hospitality, and the Jameson. Also, Captain, I've decided I agree with you about Donne. I have come to appreciate we are all part of the main. I have come to realize we do need each other. No matter how much we try to be independent and self-sustaining, it's better if we rely on one another, help each other navigate through life. The last few days have been quite eye opening. I will think of you often, Captain."

"And I of you, Christian," he says, tipping the corner of his hat.

Elan honks the horn and we look his direction. He is waving his arms pointing at his watch.

"God speed, Mister Christian."

I salute respectfully as I cross the boarding plank to shore. Before I can fasten my seatbelt, Elan shifts the jeep into gear and we pull away with a jerk. He turns on the radio to fill the dead air as we traverse the road to the airport. I adjust the volume louder.

"You like this song?"

"Yes, I guess I do," I tell him, listening to the haunting lyrics. 'No matter how far apart we are, my love, we can see the moon above. Wait for me, and you will see, I'm coming home to you.'

As the jeep rumbles along, I recall so many things I could talk about: so many people, places, and events, however, I know the retelling of my memories can never accurately convey the experiences so familiar to me, to anyone else but her. She knows me. She loves me. If anyone else except her ever read my journal entries, they would not believe it. They would scoff at my passion. They would not understand how real it is. How much I love her. They would think it some cliché pomposity: not her. She will know, she will understand.

"Thinking about Miss Lottie?" Elan asks.

"I never stop," I sigh.

Approaching the airport on the A5, we circle the roundabout and turn onto a service road. In the distance, a small flight control tower looms over an array of buildings. A variety of planes are scattered around the terminal near various hangars. After gaining permission to pass through a gateway onto the tarmac, I see the hospital emergency crew loading a gurney into the rear door of a twin-engine Piper. I notice the pilot is already onboard starting pre-flight checks. I quickly thank Elan for the ride and exit the vehicle. One of the hospital staff accompanying the patient to Liverpool opens the door to the passenger seat beside the pilot. I climb in while the others finish securing the gurney containing the feeble patient, helplessly wrapped tightly in his cotton cocoon.

"Peter. Peter Pompardinious," the pilot shouts so his voice can be heard over the roar of the twin-engines.

"Most people just call me Pete."

"Christian. John Christian. Good to meet you, Pete."

"Mister Christian, welcome aboard. Buckle up and hang on, we're cleared for immediate take-off." He speaks to the control tower through the microphone on his headset, verifying his tail number and type of aircraft. "Damn storm has moved east," he says. "Clear here. Fog and mist there. Poor visibility. I'll have to use IFR to land this baby. Man, I hate depending solely on the instruments, but you know what they say?"

"No, what?"

"Flying is the second greatest thrill known to man."

"What's the first?"

"Landing!"

Ascending quickly, we bank gently to the right over the harbor.

"Did you enjoy your time here?" he shouts.

"Yes, it's a beautiful island. Although honestly, now I'm just looking forward to getting home."

Once again, images of people and events of the past few days bombard my mind. Gil, unlucky in love for so long, now reuniting with Mary, his soul mate . . . even if he does not call it that, and Maggie his only child. I think about Cook, his tough sea-worn exterior and gruffness simply protection from the cruelness of the world. I recall the story the captain shared of his childhood, of his mother, and his grief over the recent loss of a father he barely knew. And Izaro, the proud, dying, old man, realizing his time had come to an end, wishing he had made different choices on his path. My heart feels for

Mercher losing his wife at such a young age and shutting himself off from the world all those years. And young Elan: I hope everything works out when he returns the manuscript. I remember Vikki's kind words when she spoke of Lottie and how it touched me so deeply. I reflect on the two versions of the manuscript: one full of hate and revenge, the other full of compassion and forgiveness. I wonder about Gorry, of his conflicted soul, unable to accept change; what was his choice in the end? Finally, I think of the dead man, Leece, and the ancient custom of stopping the clock at the moment of death. *Death,* I think, *did not end the love his mother and son felt for him. That will not occur until their time comes, when the hands of time are stopped for them. Life is a mystery without any certainty. Everyone walks a different path, one unique to the choices each makes. I understand now. I finally get it. Lottie was right, she always has been.*

As the plane begins to level off and the flight becomes smoother, I retrieve my journal and pen from my bag, and begin to write:

Friday, March 17, 2000

Sweetie,

I leave in haste, as I have been unable to reach you by telephone. I was offered a ride with the crew of a medical flight going to Liverpool today. I will be home soon my love. This will be my final journal entry until I see you again and share with you everything I have experienced, everything I have learned. I have so much to tell you. I pray you checked the messages and know the good news. We do have more time. We do! Please wait for me! I yearn to be with you once again, to hold you, to kiss your soft lips, to breathe in your fragrance. You are truly one of a kind: my soul mate, never to be replaced. I've been thinking a lot about our unfinished rhyme. Love does not end, not ours anyway. Like poetry, our love will transcend the years. And so, I offer you this as the perfect ending: I love you, Lottie. I always have and I always will . . . until the hands of time stand still.

Epilogue

Headline:

Six Die in Air Ambulance Crash in Liverpool

March 17, 2000—(United Press)

Six people were killed when an air ambulance en route from Isle of Man to Liverpool crashed into the River Mersey. The twin-engine Piper Navajo Chieftain light aircraft was just ten seconds away from landing at Speke Airport in Liverpool when it fell from the sky.

Two bodies were found shortly after the crash and a massive air and sea search was immediately launched for the remaining victims. Police said it would have been *'a miracle'* if any were found alive. When the tide receded, the police underwater rescue team recovered four bodies from the fuselage of the aircraft.

Investigators report the *'goldfish bowl'* effect could have been a factor and disorientated the pilot as visibility in the vicinity of Speke Airport was reduced by drizzle to 3,000 meters and the tide was *'at or about high water'* at the time of the accident.

A hospital patient, 55, who was being transferred to Liverpool for tests, was killed along with his wife, 50, the pilot, 68, the hospital deputy ward manager, 39, a 21-year-old medical student, and an unidentified male passenger. There were no survivors.

The End

Appendix

The following is a list of some of the names used in this work and information about them:

Character   Description or notes

Aine Douglas Aine was named after the Irish goddess of summer, wealth, and sovereignty. The Irish goddess was also the goddess of love and fertility, and she had command over crops and animals, and is also associated with agriculture.

Alderney   Alderney is one of the Channel Islands in the English Channel.

Andium   Andium is one of the Channel Islands in the English Channel. The name translates as "big Island."

Britannia   Britannia was the Greek and Roman term for the geographical region of Great Britain or Great Britain and Ireland. It is the name given to the female personification of the island.

buggane   Manx folklore—A shape shifter, the buggane's natural look is described as ". . .covered with a mane of coarse, black hair; it had eyes like torches, and glittering sharp tusks."

Captain   Antton is Basque for "beyond praise."
Antton Aiza   Aiza is Spanish. It means "cliff" or "rock" in
                   Basque.

Corkan   (Celtic surname) Corkan/Quirk = son of Corcan
                   (dim. of corc = heart); son of little heart.

Elan   The name Elan is of Welsh origin. The meaning of
                   Elan is "Drive, push."

Faragher   Antton is Basque for "beyond praise."Faragher
(Farmer)   was a popular surname from the Isle of Man 1881
                   census.

Father Druce   Drew — "wise." Dru, Dryw.
                   Druce — "son of Dryw." Drywsone.

Forsdal   Forsdal is the historic name for Foxdale, a village
(Farmer)   on the Isle of Man. In the 19th century there were
                   thirteen mines and workings in the area of
                   Foxdale, which included five mines working the
                   Foxdale shear. The mines yielded a rich output of
                   zinc blend, lead ore and silver.

Gorry's Father Also referred to as "Fides," which is Latin for trust,
(Ghost)   faith, belief.

Gorry's Mother Called Iniuria, which is Latin for injury, offense,
(Ghost)   injustice, wrongdoing.

Gowerr Mercher Gowerr — "pure."

Mercher — Welsh form of Mercury, Roman
messenger of the gods.

Hibernia   Hibernia is the classical Latin name for the island
of Ireland.

Iniko   Iniko is an African prince who deeply loved the
(See also Risi)   beautiful Folami. His name means "time of
trouble."

Izaro Ander   (Captain's father) Izaro: Basque name meaning
(Old Man)   "island."

Ander—Basque form of Andrew, which refers to
man, or manly.

Justus   Named after JESUS JUSTUS, je'-zus jus'-tus
(The little   Iesous ho legomenos Ioustos, "Jesus that is called
blind boy)   Justus," (Colossians 4:11) The name Justus is a
Biblical baby name. The name Justus is: Just or
upright.

Leece   (Celtic surname) Leece = Son of the
Servant/Devotee of Jesus, inheritance.

Lottie   Appears in three characters. She is spiritual, kind,
and loving—as defined by the protagonist
Christian in our outer story; she is Mona—the
desire of Gorry; and she is Aine—the thoughtful
and wise heroine of the inner book.

Mona

The name Mona is the Latinized form that would correspond to the name Man. Mona is the female form/name for Man (as in Isle of Man).

Pretani people

In the 1st century BCE, the Pretani people inhabited the British Isles.

Prettanike (Latin) (Mona's adopted father)

Prettanike is a word that originally designated a collection of islands with individual names, including Great Britain.

Risi (see also Iniko)

Old Norse nickname for giant.

Saoi

The word saoi is used in Irish meaning wise man.

Sark

Sark is one of the Channel Islands in the English Channel.

Spirit of Man

The Spirit of Man haunts lonely places and waterfalls, and, according to his mood, helps or harms the wayfarer. His appearance is that of a man with shaggy hair and beard.